Please review on Goodreads.com

# Tiger
### and the
# Robot

GRAHAME SHANNON

Copyright © 2016 Grahame Shannon
All rights reserved.

Print Edition:
ISBN: 1541281594
ISBN-13: 978-1541281592

# DEDICATION

To Kathleen, James, and Shirley

# CONTENTS

Dedication .................................................. iii

Contents ..................................................... v

Acknowledgements ....................................... i

Prologue ..................................................... 1

1 The Race Underground ............................. 4

2 Dream wheels ........................................ 10

3 Building Birdhouses ............................... 22

4 Waiting for Sunrise ................................ 27

5 The Code Book for Young People ........... 40

6 Destined to Meet .................................... 50

7 The Gang That Wouldn't Write Straight .... 56

8 The Will of the Empress ......................... 60

9 The Room .............................................. 68

10 Tiger's Voyage ..................................... 82

11 Searching for Dragons .......................... 87

12 By the Sword ....................................... 97

13 Turtle in Paradise ............................... 105

14 Almost a Family ................................ 115

15 I Am a Japanese Writer ...................... 124

16 Flight of Dreams ................................ 128

17 All Our Happy Days Are Stupid ..................... 132

18 I Have No Mouth and I Must Scream ............ 140

19 Under the Jolly Roger ...................................... 149

20 This Changes Everything ................................ 166

21 The Hollow Chocolate Bunnies of the
Apocalypse ......................................................... 178

22 The Double Comfort Safari Club ................... 186

23 The Gods of Newport ..................................... 196

24 Follow the Money ........................................... 200

25 Where the Wild Things Are ............................ 212

26 Stage Fright on a Summer Night .................... 231

27 Prisoner of Night and Fog ............................... 241

28 The Restaurant at the End of the Universe ..... 256

Epilogue ............................................................... 259

Note ...................................................................... 260

About the Author ................................................. 262

# ACKNOWLEDGEMENTS

Thank you to the friends who helped me by reading and criticizing many drafts. Special thanks to Michael McGrath, David Eaman, Pierre Cote, Bill Trant, and Christopher Paton-Gay.

Fellow members of the Federation of BC Writers, especially Ellen Niemer, Alexander Boldizar and Ray Wood have also offered suggestions and advice for which I'm deeply grateful.

General thanks to Google, Wikipedia, and Bing for providing vital research tools and information.

Technical inaccuracies are mine and mine alone.

# PROLOGUE

In 1716 an Edo craftsman named Moriyama created a mechanical fortune-telling machine called Gokensuki. It was a lacquered wood box about the size of a human head. The box had carved, painted eyes and nose on the front and lifelike carved ears on the sides. There was a flap below the nose, painted to look like a mouth, which opened when a lever on the right side was pressed.

It sat on a draped table. The operator would sweep the draping open on request to show there was nothing underneath.

The operator would collect a fee, then write down a short question requested by the client. He would place the slip of paper on the table facing Gokensuki. After a short delay, he would press the lever and Gokensuki would spit out a written answer in the form of a Haiku.

History has not recorded the questions asked or Gokensuki's responses, save one. In 1718 the Emperor of Japan heard of the device and demanded to have it and Moriyama brought to court for a demonstration.

When the event came, the room was cleared. The Emperor brought a question already written on a piece of parchment and placed it on the table in front of Gokensuki. He waited the prescribed time but insisted on pressing the lever himself. When he read the resulting haiku, he became apoplectic. The machine was ordered destroyed and Moriyama was beheaded. This is what he read:

*Ten thousand blossoms*

*Clouds thunder in from the east*

*A few sticks remain*

In December of 1941, the Japanese Navy staged a daring attack on Pearl Harbor, Hawaii, main Pacific base of the US Navy. This triggered the entry of the US into World War Two. In mid-1942 Japanese Navy planes twice bombed and shelled Dutch Harbor, Alaska.

A few days later Japanese forces invaded and occupied Attu and Kiska islands in the Aleutians, apparently to prevent a US attack on the Japanese Kuril Islands. Eventually, 5200 men were garrisoned on Kiska. In October 1942, the US bombed Kiska several times. On August 15, 1943, a combined US and Canadian force of 34,426 troops invaded Kiska to drive out the Japanese. No Japanese were found and it was discovered that they had left on June 28 under cover of heavy fog. Despite that, more than 200 Allied troops were killed by booby traps, friendly fire, and unfriendly weather.

When US troops arrived in nearby Little Kiska Island, again, no Japanese were found. Reportedly the only things that remained on the island were dogs and freshly brewed coffee. Asked for an explanation, the reporting officer replied, "The Japanese are very clever. Their dogs can brew coffee."

An American propaganda leaflet in the shape of a kiri leaf found on Kiska:

## TIGER AND THE ROBOT

*Before spring comes a second time*
*American bombs*
*like Kiri leaves falling far away*
*will bring sadness and misfortune*

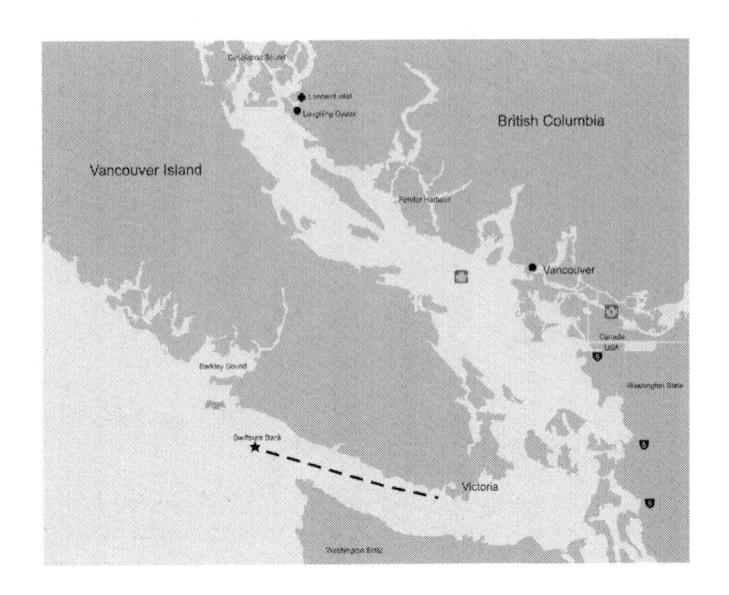

Map of Swiftsure Racecourse

# 1 THE RACE UNDERGROUND

I woke up alone in the big bed of the Royal Suite at the Empress. There was a note on the bed beside me.

*"Thanks for a wonderful night. See you on board. Gina."*

I had forgotten that I was supposed to sail on Aphrodite in the Swiftsure Race. It was just before eight. I jumped out of bed, found my duffel bag and pulled on my sailing clothes. No breakfast for this boy.

I barely made it to the boat before it left the dock. Somebody had brought a box of Timbits on board so I gobbled a few, along with a cup of coffee in a foam cup. Then I helped the rest of the crew run the sheets and ready the headsails.

*The Swiftsure International Yacht Race is the premier long distance sailing race in the Pacific Northwest and British Columbia area. Starting and ending in Victoria, BC, Canada, the Swiftsure is international because the midpoint markers for the four long courses are in U.S. waters. Organized by the Royal Victoria Yacht Club, the race occurs during the Memorial Day weekend in May with staggered starts on Saturday morning. The race is most popular with sailors from British Columbia and Washington, but it has drawn boats from as far away as California, Hawaii, New Zealand, and even Russia. -Wikipedia*

At 120 feet, the Aphrodite—the crew called her Afro—was the biggest boat in the race. Gina wasn't aboard, and the skipper told me she got an urgent call and took off for Rio in her private jet. I had never felt so disappointed in my life. I tried not to think about her as we got ready to sail. The big diesel rumbled to life and deckhands freed the mooring lines. The bow thruster whirred loudly as it pushed us away from the dock. We threaded our way out of the long narrow harbor, dodging tugs, seaplanes, and dozens of other yachts heading for the starting line.

"All Cell Phones off." someone said. No distractions during the race. I switched mine off.

The skipper, Billy Taylor, took the wheel at the start. The tactician, whose name I didn't get, called the position time to the line. Two lookouts watched for crossing boats. The warning signal went at 8.51 AM. It was nine minutes to the start. Billy held back until one minute before the gun, so it seemed most of the boats in our start—the first—were ahead of us. Then he spun the wheel and shouted.

"Go for it!"

The crew sprang into action. Two gorillas cranked the coffee-grinder sheet winch at amazing speed. The big carbon fiber genoa filled with a crack and Afro leaped ahead, exceeding ten knots before we crossed the line. The wake hissed and roared. When the starting signal blew, we were about third, but moving faster than the other boats, all of them much smaller except the Oriole, the Canadian Navy's antique training yacht. Within a few minutes, we were leading the race.

We beat to windward toward the Swiftsure Bank, a shallow area off the west coast of Vancouver Island. There used to be a Lightship there, but it had been replaced with an automated buoy.

Despite the strong wind, Aphrodite heeled only about ten degrees. Changing tacks, which we did every five miles or so, the huge electric sheet winches reeled in the sheets at great speed. The crew worked together like a well-oiled machine. On deck, the apparent wind—the wind you felt onboard—was fierce as we sailed into it at over twelve knots. We easily led the fleet all the way to the buoy.

We rounded the windward mark at Swiftsure Bank at about 8 PM. There were no other boats in sight, so Billy left plenty of room. The jib furled in smoothly and moments later the colorful spinnaker filled with a snap, and billowed out ahead. It was the biggest sail I had ever seen.

Billy asked me to take over the steering on the downwind leg. Afro had twin wheels, each well to one side, so the helmsman could see the sails. I was holding the port wheel. Billy was at the other wheel, hands off. Steering took all my concentration and other thoughts left my head. There was a tremendous feeling of power, as the big carbon fiber wheel slid through my hands. Each time there was a gust of wind I had to apply more rudder to compensate.

At sea, steering a yacht, nothing else existed. The wind, the waves, the shape of the sails, and the rudder's tug in my palms became my entire world. Even Gina fell to the back of my mind as I gave it my full concentration.

As we raced to the finish the wind increased steadily. Halfway back, Afro was making nearly 25 knots over the bottom in a wind of 35 knots or so. The sky ahead was aglow with the promise of early dawn. As we passed Race Rocks there was a sudden gust of wind and the boat began to round up to port. I spun the wheel, but she heeled so far over the rudder stalled and lost its grip. As we broached, all hell broke loose. Lines were flailing around. Shouts of fear and advice rang out. Waves were washing into the cockpit. I was paralyzed and useless, hanging on for dear life, since the wheel did nothing.

The tactician shouted. "Let the sheets fly!"

When the mainsheet was let go it whistled through the blocks and the boom crashed against the rigging. The boat was so far over the lee winches were underwater and the crew couldn't free the spinnaker sheet.

My senses returned and I shouted, "Let the guy off."

Letting the spinnaker guy fly in those conditions could bring down the mast when the pole hit the forestay. That would cause devastating damage, and probably some injuries or even deaths. The crew member on the line looked at Billy.

"Do it!" he screamed.

When the line let go, the huge carbon spinnaker pole flew forward and crashed against the forestay, where it splintered and bent in two. The spinnaker lost its wind and flew flapping from the masthead. The boat came upright, slowly, water pouring off the decks and out through the open transom. When the rudder regained grip, I steered back to the proper course and the crew trimmed the main. Soon we were sailing at a sedate ten knots or so as the crew wrestled the torn spinnaker down and shoved it through the hatch.

Billy took over the steering. Soon they brought out a smaller asymmetric spinnaker, which set without a pole. With that up, we continued to the finish line at speeds as much as 20 knots. A glowing wake streamed out behind us as we sailed toward the dawn.

I figured that carbon fiber pole must have cost as much as my boat, but the crew wasn't upset about breaking it. It wasn't their money.

When we crossed the finish line, the committee boat fired a gun and blew a horn. People on board waved and clapped. Our crew shouted with joy and high-fives were exchanged. It was just past 2 AM Sunday. The next boat in our division was still three hours behind. The other boats would be finishing throughout the day.

It took about 15 minutes to get the sails down and stowed, and start the engine. By 3 AM we were tied up in the empty marina in front of the Empress. The crew took off their foul weather gear. The sound of champagne corks was heard.

I tried to call Gina, but her cell phone was off. Rio was a long way from BC, so I thought she might still be flying. As the onboard victory celebration party was winding down, Billy came over with an anxious look on his face.

"The pilot just called me. My phone was off during the race. He waited all day at the Victoria airport, and Gina never showed. I just assumed that she was well on her way. I called her cell, but it's off. I left a message, but so far, no callback. Did she say anything last night that gives you an idea what happened?"

I took a moment to think over what she had said, but I kept remembering what we'd done. "No. I didn't see her yesterday at all."

.

## 2 DREAM WHEELS

Nine months earlier:

It started with a dream...

I dreamt in the language of the moment. In engineering school, my dreams were filled with strange and wonderful machines. Learning to cook, exotic foods prevailed. Starting to sail, I dreamed in air and water flow over foils and appendages. Three-dimensional and fully colored, in a way that no drawing could equal.

Teaching myself computer programming I dreamt in Fortran, later Basic and Java. Nightmares were in C++.

Mostly I forgot the dreams, though they were incredibly vivid. Occasionally, with a dream fresh in memory, I'd jot down the highlights. A pad and pen lived by the bed just for that.

One morning in 2015, I woke up to this note:

*Siri. Cortana. Sherlock.*

That's all. I knew that Siri was Apple's personal digital assistant. Cortana was Microsoft's lesser-known equivalent. And Sherlock must have referred to Sherlock Holmes, Sir Arthur Conan Doyle's fictional detective. Perhaps my subconscious was telling me to develop an app that would perform the functions of a detective? I liked the idea, primarily to stave off boredom and prevent me from ruminating on past failures.

My name is Chandler Gray, but my friends call me

Chan. I had just come off a three-year stint as president of an app development start-up. From rags to riches and back to rags…but that was another story.

Anyway, I had time on my hands, and enough money left to live for a year or two, in my somewhat frugal way. Did I mention that I lived on a boat?

A Hinckley Bermuda 40, a millionaire's yacht, with gleaming chrome and polished teak everywhere. At least that's how she would have looked when she was new, about fifty years ago. I picked her up at A-1 auctions.

She was a classic yacht, with plenty of storage. The previous owner found room for a large bale of marijuana in the lazarette and five kilos of coke in the bilge. Canada Customs lacked an appreciation of such things. The owner skipped.

She was called Blue Rose. I liked the name, and anyway, it was carved right into the transom. Changing it would cost money. In those days, she could have used some cosmetics, and the sails were tired, but the Perkins diesel ran well and the hull was sound. I planned to restore her when I could afford it.

In the chilly dawn, I climbed out of the vee-berth and pulled on a sweat suit. The Force Ten propane stove hissed gently as I put on the kettle. I would make coffee with a Bodum French press, no electricity needed.

While I waited for the kettle I thought about the feasibility of a detective app.

I envisaged a perfect detective's assistant. She'd have long wavy blonde hair, a short skirt, and curves in all the right places. She'd have a genius IQ, know how to hack and code, and be available at all hours. Now, make her into a robot. Sadly, I mentally removed her body, leaving a phone app.

Robots existed, even fairly lifelike robots. None of them could move like a human, independent of a power source for more than a few minutes. I had been in the hardware business before. It sucked. This time everything would be software, and using hardware that was already widespread. A smartphone would work for a user interface, but serious processing power would be needed. The Cloud was the place for that.

It couldn't be an iPhone app. Apple kept too tight a control on app capabilities. I already knew how to program for Android and Windows. I picked Android because I had a couple of Android phones and all the development tools left over from my last venture. Also, Android was open source, and it was possible to modify the operating system if it somehow stood in the way.

Friends said I was obsessive. Once I grabbed onto an idea, I would lunge headlong into it, full speed ahead and damn the torpedoes. So it was with the Sherlock application.

I began by texting my buddy N. Eli Feinman. He was a hacker extraordinaire with friends in both high and low places. Outwardly he gave the appearance of being a somewhat aimless dilettante. Not true. He had a very quick mind and deep wells of arcane knowledge about circuitry and anything with wires. He collected antique cameras—the kind that used film—and old oscilloscopes.

# TIGER AND THE ROBOT

I texted: *Siri. Cortana. Sherlock.*

In seconds a reply came back. *Wilder Snail. 30 minutes.*

I had to Google the place. It was a couple of blocks south of the Maker Lab where Feinman maintained his workspace.

After changing into chinos, a yellow collared shirt, and Topsiders, I walked up the floating dock to where my car was parked in an old loading bay. A great car, another classic. A 1965 Mustang convertible. They could go for fifty grand at auction in Las Vegas. Okay, maybe mine wasn't quite that good. Fine, a long way from that good, but I planned to restore it to top shape soon. In the meantime, the duct tape kept out the rain and Frank had welded the muffler back on. Again.

I pulled the orange tarp off the car and rolled it up. It started after only a bit of hesitation. The drive was only a few blocks and I found a street parking spot. Meters were cheaper on the east side of town. A toonie—the Canadian two-dollar coin—got me an hour.

The Wilder Snail was a small corner grocery store with a coffee bar. Hip young people sold organic groceries and served good bevies. The tables had three legs and didn't wobble. I appreciated the kind of owner who would think of that. The place had attitude.

Feinman and I had been best friends since High School. I could talk to him without fear of anything except gossip. Anyway, it was a give and take situation.

He was a bit late, as usual. I already had a coffee and a muffin in front of me when he dropped his bike helmet and man-purse (which he claimed was an iPad case) on the table and went for a bagel sandwich.

He brought me up to date on his various neurotic friends, some of whom I knew. I guess I was one of them, and he probably updated the others on my antics too. He was always careful not to reveal anything private, like their bank account numbers and email passwords, even though I was pretty sure he knew them.

"I have an idea for an app." I jumped in as he took a sip of his coffee. We batted ideas back and forth all the time. Most of the time we were trying to figure out how to take advantage of stupid people with money. There was a major oversupply of them in Vancouver. A lesser theme was how middle-aged guys could attract younger women.

"Another app? There are already millions of them. Let me guess. It's a robot detective running on a smartphone." He had deciphered my cryptic text correctly.

"Yes, almost. It should really be called Watson since it is an assistant to a live investigator. Unfortunately, IBM already uses that name. I'll need your help to make it work."

"Is this a commercial venture or a labor of love?"

"I'm interested in developing the technology. It's too sensitive to sell. I already got burned by pirate copies of my last app. This one will be privately distributed."

"What do you need my help for? You're the

programmer." He had a pretty good idea what I would want, but I'd need to beg a bit.

"It will be an AI app." AI was the acronym for Artificial Intelligence. I often derided AI by calling it Artificial Stupidity, but even I had to admit that it had reached the point where it could be useful. I lowered my voice. "A phone isn't powerful enough, I'll need a back-end server with lots of storage and multiple fast CPUs. And, I'll need your help for access to certain databases."

He looked over his shoulder to see who was listening. Nobody. "I never do anything that's illegal—in Antarctica. But I have a buddy who over-invested in server hardware. Can you afford a hundred a month?"

"Sure. All I have to do is stop buying you coffee." I did sometimes pay, but so did Feinman.

"Okay. Give me a business card, and I'll have him call you." He smirked, knowing I didn't have a card right then.

"You know the info. Just email it. The project will need untraceable access to a few things. Not saying what they are now, but I'll send you an encrypted list." I didn't want to verbalize that bit, just in case. Feinman nodded and we stepped outside. He pulled on his helmet, climbed on his bike and headed for the lab, I went around the corner to my car.

On my way back to the boat, I began to design the app in my head. First would be the back end, which would be a query engine, accessing a variety of databases, public and private. Facebook, Twitter, Google Plus and other social networks were on the list. And of course, it could use search sites including

Google, Bing, and Yahoo.

It would need access to credit card statements, phone records, criminal records, license plate numbers, surveillance cameras, and a few other things that civilians and even most police are not supposed to access, at least without a warrant. I was certain that Feinman knew ways to get that information. We would set up a double firewall so my server app could get the information without revealing the source, or the fact that we had accessed it.

The "front end" app would run on the phone. There would be a minimal user interface, just speech and text. It would send encrypted queries to the "back end", and display or speak the answers. The real heavy duty processing would be in the cloud, and that was where 90% of my coding time would be spent.

I would need a place to work, apart from my boat. Partly because of security. Boats were very easy to break into. Another reason was that I wanted to be able to get away from work sometimes, and that was hard when you lived in the office.

A couple of blocks up from the dock was a local coffee shop, the Clever Café. It was a small place on the ground floor of an old stucco-faced building. It was one star short of a Starbucks, but I liked the coffee, and they let me run a tab. I actually named the place. They were looking for a clever name and I suggested the obvious. It stuck.

Outside the neighborhood was a little rough, with litter around, sometimes needles. There were often a few seedy drunks sitting around on the bench by the bus stop, with bottles in paper bags. It wasn't a major street, but only one block off East Hastings, which was. Safe enough, at least in the daytime, as the bums were too hung over to be dangerous, and the drug dealers and pimps didn't come out until after dark. A beat cop walked by at least once an hour.

I parked the car at the dock, got the orange tarp out and dragged it over the leaky convertible top. I strolled up to the Clever.

Xena, the owner, had seen me coming across the street and already had my long espresso ready. She even added the tiny bit of milk I like. Xena is attractive in a tall, full figured athletic way, with flaming red hair and a pale complexion accented by a light sprinkle of freckles. She pitches for an alternative team so flirting is wasted. I took my coffee and sat down at a window table. I was the only client at the time so I motioned her over to join me. She grabbed a bottle of water and sat opposite me.

"How come bottled water is evil, but Pepsi is cool?" Xena had an inventory of one-liners that she recycled regularly.

"Do you still have that room upstairs for rent?"

"Yeah, but it's, like, a suite. Got a shower and everything. I've been asking $300, but so far no takers."

"$300 a month? Sounds fair." A bargain. I was expecting double that.

"You dork! Don't you have any idea of Vancouver rents? $300 a week. That's W-E-E-K." She got up and took a key off a hook behind the bar. Tossing it to me she said, "Have a look."

The key missed my hand and I had to fish around

on the floor with a foot, then bend over to pick it up. My back creaked painfully. Nothing to do with my age, but I probably needed to work out more. Or at all.

The steep, well-worn, wooden stairs creaked and groaned as I climbed them. The hand rail was loose. The door at the top was painted white but yellowed and peeling with age. Above the door was an old-fashioned transom vent, with a pane of cracked glass. So far so good.

I had to push the door hard and the rusty hinges squealed in protest. A little oil would soon put that right. There were a combined living room and kitchen, a bedroom and a bathroom. The galley was just a counter with a chipped enamel sink, a one burner hot plate, and a bar sized fridge. None of it was new. A massive oak desk almost filled the living room, which had a single small window. An old wooden swivel chair with a blue foam pad was semi-comfortable. There were two rusty steel folding chairs which had once been painted gray. A dented beige 3 drawer file cabinet with a broken lock stood beside the desk. It was perfect!

The bedroom was small, maybe eight feet square. There was an old-fashioned brass bedstead with a single mattress. The mattress had to go. It looked and smelled as if something—or someone—had died on it. The 3-drawer chest was made of cheap pine, and the front was hanging off the bottom drawer. The bathroom had a toilet, a sink, and a shower. It was about the same size as the head on my boat, but not as well finished. There were two electrical outlets in the front room and one in the back. Not nearly enough for my purposes, but I knew an electrician who worked cheap.

There was a shortage of rental space in Vancouver, so I knew the place must be lacking, and Xena didn't have other dorks lined up to rent it. Back downstairs I tossed the key to Xena. "I'll give you $800 a month for it. And I promise to fix it up some."

She snorted. "You've got a fucking nerve. I wouldn't rent it to a jerk like you for twice that."

After we traded a few more insults we settled on $900 and I gave her a check for the first and last month. "When can I move in?"

"I'll give you the keys as soon as the check clears." Xena smiled—but it wasn't a very trusting smile. I might have bounced a check on her once or twice…

A couple of days later I got possession and I texted my sailing buddy Olivier.

*Can you meet me at the Clever?*

*He replied: 2 PM.*

Ollie owned a sign shop, but he could build just about anything. He also had a designer's eye for attractive and functional decor. It was a rare combination and he had helped me with several projects.

He showed up in a Ferrari Red Ferrari. An older F355. Without looking I knew it had a manual transmission. Ollie was a purist, who didn't believe in automatic anything. He was a few inches shorter than my six one and a little younger, with a jolly face and thinning light brown hair. He was originally a French kid from Montreal, but his family moved to Vancouver when he was ten. Still had a slight French accent but his English was otherwise excellent. He could be charming, or sarcastic, depending on the occasion.

I stepped outside to look at the car and help him out of the ultra-low driver's seat. "Found another way to deplete your ill-gotten gains?"

"I wrote off my Lotus on the Sea-to-Sky highway near Whistler. I was drifting through a corner on the perfect line, when suddenly the rear end swung right into the center barricade. Then it bounced off and spun. It wasn't my fault. Mechanical failure. Tie-rod broke in the rear suspension. This is just a loaner until I get paid by the insurance."

"Wow. They usually give me a Toyota Yaris—if I'm lucky."

"Tough. I know you prefer rusty antiques."

"That's why I hang around with you."

"Hey, that hurts," Ollie said with a grin. "Let's have a look at this dump."

We spent a few minutes upstairs looking over the place, and he snapped some photos with his phone. Then we went down to the Clever to discuss it over coffee.

"I want to keep the grubby-chic look," I said.

"Is that what you call it? I'd call it 60's Cockroach. Or maybe Miami Lice."

"Whatever. Here are my needs. I want to conceal a powerful PC in the desk. Make the top lift with a big LCD monitor on the underside, and hide the computer on the right behind the drawers. Ideally, the AC power would come up through one of the legs.

When it's closed, I want it to look like an old wooden desk, nothing more. Bolted to the floor." His eyes rolled upward at the request.

"Why the secrecy? Nobody steals PCs anymore, just laptops and tablets." Ollie could do what I needed, he just wanted to know why.

"I'm starting a new project, and it is kind of sensitive." I trusted Ollie with my life, but not my wallet. Anyway, I gave him an abbreviated description of the project, and he got it right away.

I said, "I know you can keep a secret, otherwise your wife would have found out already."

"Found out what?"

"Exactly. Anyway, what do you think?"

"Okay, the gray Lino on the floor has to go. We'll pull it up and put new wiring under there. High-speed internet and encrypted Wi-Fi. I'll find some old fir flooring that will look original. We'll steam clean everything, then repaint it. After that, we'll distress it. I'll modify the desk at my shop. You'll owe me big time for this."

"Thanks. How soon..."

# 3 BUILDING BIRDHOUSES

A couple of weeks after I first mentioned the office I got a call from Ollie. I had given him a key to the place and figured he was calling to tell me the job was done.

"Hi Chan. About the office. I should be able to get started next week. I had a cancellation from a drug dealer who wanted his store renovated."

Knowing Ollie, I figured he was talking about a pharmacy. But in Vancouver, it could be a Medical Marijuana dispensary. Or a Vape shop.

I wasn't too pleased. I told him, "I'm not too pleased. I thought you would be done by now. Wait…I know, paying customers have priority. How about if we work together on it?"

We agreed on the following Tuesday morning, and he gave me a list of materials to buy. He'd bring his work truck, a white Ford Transit, with the tools we'd need.

Since our previous meeting my tech buddy Feinman and I had spent a lot of time together, and he introduced me to some Russian hackers on the Dark Net. I got the connections and servers set up at very reasonable cost, and paid in Bitcoin. We took to communicating only in person, by passing an iPad back and forth. However, by the time I heard from Ollie I had written an email encryption app which I reckoned was very, very hard to crack without the 256-bit key. Only Feinman and I had it. The key changed daily in an automated way, so a hacker would have to be nimble to crack it. Paranoia? Maybe. But anyway, we could email back and forth without fear. We used two different email accounts each so the reply was always sent from a different account from the one that received it. More paranoia.

Anyone with even an inkling about computer programming would know the task I had set myself was a gargantuan one. There is only one way a lone programmer could create an app like that in a lifetime. So, I did what I had done many times before on big projects. I cheated.

Truly dedicated programmers liked to hand craft every line of code. Cheaters like me bought or licensed libraries. There were thousands of libraries of code to do almost anything you could imagine. IBM had a service in the Watson Cloud that transformed speech into text with amazing accuracy. Ivona Speech Cloud went the other way, text to speech. This was important because I didn't want to type much, and the app needed to communicate with me when my hands were full.

I decided to call the persona of the app Saga (pronounced Say-gah) after the Malmo detective in the Swedish TV series the Bridge. I loved that character.

I didn't end up dealing with IBM or anyone else offering an internet service for speech, but I found similar code I could buy and run on my "own" servers in Russia. That way a third party couldn't listen to Saga's conversations.

Basically, in two weeks, with an outlay of cash of way less than the down payment on a studio apartment in Yaletown, I had about 90% of the functions I needed to bring Saga to life. I chose a middle-class British accent for her, after sampling 50 or 60 "text to speech" voices. Test sentences came out very well, not much like a robot, and I found punctuation such as a question mark, elicited the correct inflection.

I was left without the two major chunks of code which would be the "brains" of the app. These would be a Correlation Engine—looking for connections between events, things, and people—and an Inference Engine. The latter would be used to divine meaning from correlations. Of course, there was a bunch of minor housekeeping code to put it all together. I figured two or three weeks max. Then I remembered an old software development rule. Take your best estimate and double it. Then double it again, and you might be close to right. So, twelve weeks was my completion target. If I knew how long it would actually take, I might not have started.

Ollie and I managed to rip up the floor, rewire the place, modify the desk, including hidden armor plate, and a long list of other tasks, in six days, six bottles of Pinot Noir, and twelve steaks. Not to mention a few gallons of espresso. Every day when we couldn't do more we'd retreat to a place Ollie built and once owned. Grape Expectations.

It was a cozy wine bar, mostly wine by the glass, but the food was passable. The décor was kind of 80s mahogany and black granite, but still cool, and there was a lot of eye candy around. I liked it okay, and it was just a few blocks west of my office. The music was loud enough so we could talk shop without fear of being overheard. On the last day of the reno, Ollie showed me something.

"Look behind the bar while the bartender is in the

back. Let me know what you spot." I think he was testing my detective skills. I held my phone behind the bar and snapped a photo. More reliable than a memory.

I had a look. Almost immediately I spotted two taps. One was marked RED and the other was marked WHITE. 28 different white wines, 32 reds, and a few rosés by the glass were on the menu. I held up the photo and cocked a questioning eyebrow.

"Oui. Just two taps. A bit of each and you have a rose. Add a bit of lemon to the white and you have Pinot Grigio. A bit of Cherry Coke in the red and you have a Cabernet. It's the only way to make money in a place like this. Now you know why I always order a bottle." And I thought it was because I was paying. Silly me.

"By the way, I think insurance is going to write off the Lotus. The repair estimate came in at almost the price of a new one. Mine was four years old, so they will probably give me about a third as much," Ollie whined. Probably still enough for a brand-new Mercedes. I'd miss the screaming silver beast, and the exercise I got rolling my large frame over the absurdly high and wide door sill into the passenger seat.

"Vultures are circling the wreck out back of the dealer. One guy wants the engine; another wants the transaxle. These people have no respect for the newly dead. The oil is probably still warm."

"So you'll be shopping for a new car. What will you get this time?" I hoped it might be something easier on my back.

"I haven't decided yet, but not a Lotus. It attracted too much attention." Ollie smiled sadly.

"I thought you liked the attention."

"Not from people carrying guns…" I hoped he meant the police.

When we parted I promised to give him a demo of the app in a few weeks. The next day I made the same promise to Feinman. Oddly they both had the same response.

"Bullshit!"

Oh, ye of little faith.

# 4 WAITING FOR SUNRISE

After two months of work hooking things together and writing code, I had a text version of Saga ready for testing. I started with very basic stuff.

*What is your name?*

*My name is Saga.*

*What's up, Saga?*

*I don't know what is up.*

*What do you know?*

*My name is Saga.*

There was no doubting it was robotic. In order to give more interesting answers, the app would have to remember previous questions. It would need multiple phrases to be used randomly for answering similar questions.

After another month or so I tried again.

*What is your name?*

*My name is Saga. What's yours?*

*I'm Chandler Gray, but you can call me Chan.*

*Nice to meet you is Chandler Gray, but you can call me Chan.*

*What do you know?*

*I already told you my name. Your name is Chandler Gray, but you can call me Chan. It is a long name.*

Progress had been made. But, the name thing

needed work. And she didn't know much. I quit work on the intelligence to spent some time on the speech recognition and spoken responses.

For a month, I read the leading article in the Vancouver Sun to the app daily, after correcting the typos. Each time it failed to recognize a word, I added it to the speech dictionary and recorded my way of saying it. Gradually the accuracy of recognition improved until it was better than 99%. However, that level only applied when I was the one talking. Playing the CBC news on the radio, about 92% was recognized.

Sometimes I would have the app read the transcribed text back to me. It worked well from the start, and with tweaks, it began to be hard to tell from a live person. Still, you wouldn't hire Saga as a news reader.

I tried the basic tests using voice. I had also added some M2M (machine to machine) functions, such as the ability to autonomously place and answer phone calls and text messages. Saga was allowed full use of Google and Wikipedia.

"Saga, what's my name?" I programmed it so you had to say her name to start a conversation or give a command.

"Chan."

"Saga, what is my full name."

"Chandler Gray."

"Saga, what's up?"

"Today, the Dow Jones index is up. The temperature in Vancouver is up. My server is up."

I had limited her to three items in such a reply, otherwise, she could go for hours. There was a random factor introduced, so if you asked the same question twice, you'd get a different answer.

"Saga, can you find me a restaurant nearby that's open for lunch?"

"According to Yelp, there are eight restaurants within one kilometer open for lunch. They are…" She gave the full list.

I would have to teach her my food preferences. I needed to add Machine Learning code, so she could learn new facts or behavior verbally. I wanted no more than three responses to a question like that.

Several months later…

What a big job it was. I had hardly lifted my hands off the keyboard since the office was finished. My social life—never exactly vibrant—was down to zero. Even my closest friends hadn't seen much of me, although we had talked and texted a bit.

Saga was working reasonably well. She was definitely superior to Siri. However, there was some refinement still needed. I tried a quick start up. The phone booted up, and displayed a brief magnifying glass icon, indicating my app was active, then reverted to the standard Android screen.

"Good morning, Saga." Her name could come at either end of a command.

"Greetings all powerful one. I am ready to do your every bidding." That sounded good although not quite what was expected.

"Saga, I am going to take a coffee break."

"According to Google, you should take your break at McDonald's, Apparently, they have a triple-bacon cheeseburger on special. They will super-size your fries."

I opened the server code and removed Google as the default search engine and replaced it with DuckDuckGo. It didn't track users and allowed you to disable advertising. Which I did. This took only five minutes.

"Saga, will you get me a coffee? Long espresso with just a bit of milk." I didn't program anything like that, but the app was supposed to deal with any request.

"Coming right up. Calling the Clever Café." Xena picked up on the third ring.

"Clever Café."

"Xena, this is Saga, Chandler Gray's personal assistant. Will you bring up his morning coffee? "

Xena's reply was unprintable. She hung up. To be fair to Saga, if I called the result would have been the same.

"You must go down and get it yourself, Oh Mighty One."

"Thanks for trying Saga, but just call me Chan."

This was a breakthrough. I decided to do a field test. I called up Charlie Quant, another friend. Charlie lives in Southlands, where he keeps a stable. No horses, just a collection of antique cars. I hadn't told him about Saga, so I figured he'd be good to try it out on. He was in his shop and invited me to come over for coffee. It was about thirty minutes away from my office.

I pulled the orange tarp off the Mustang, and after a few coughs and farts—the car, not me—it started up. I put the phone on the passenger seat.

"Saga, get me directions to Charlie Quant's place." I knew the way but this was a test. The app was in debug mode so I would get extra comments as it went.

"Looking for Charlie Quant in contacts. Found." The female British accent sounded just right. Friendly but efficient.

"Email, phone number but no street address. Initiating reverse lookup. Unlisted number. Stealth checking." There was a brief pause then, "Found address. Activating Google Maps."

Google maps started giving me driving directions in a different voice, Saga had done "her" job perfectly. In a couple of blocks, I got tired of listening to directions I didn't need.

"Saga, deactivate Google Maps."

"Yes, Master." It was Barbara Eden's voice, of the old *I Dream of Jeannie* TV series. I didn't remember programming that. Anyway, Google stopped.

I tried another function. "Saga, what is the traffic like on Granville street south of Broadway?"

"Checking traffic cameras. Slow from Broadway to 16th avenue but no obstructions. Stalled car in the right lane just before 41st avenue. A green Jaguar XJ6 with vanity plate 600BJS." Her own voice was back.

"Thanks, Saga, you don't need to describe the vehicles in a traffic check unless asked."

"Jawohl, Mein Fuhrer." Marlene Dietrich voice, followed by a click of heels. I was damn sure I would have remembered programming that. The machine learning functions seemed to work, but not quite as I had imagined. Neural networks can be unpredictable.

Saga had unlimited access to the internet, but I had made a list of trusted sites and databases that could be used for informational research. I didn't want her to give me fake info, and the internet is full of that. She could access music and videos. She must have grabbed some audio clips for the voices. Probably a copyright violation...

When we got to Charlie's his electric gate was closed. There was an intercom there but I thought I'd try out another capability.

"Saga, can you open Charlie's gate?"

"Checking. It is network controlled. Hacking Wi-Fi. In. Yes, I can open the gate." Nothing happened. I waited a few seconds.

"Saga, please open the gate." Apparently, she was fussy about grammar.

"Open Sesame!" The Barbara Eden voice was followed by the twinkling sound that accompanied magic in the show. The gate slid open.

I drove around the back where the stables were. Charlie came out of the open door. I slipped the phone into the pocket of my windbreaker. He was a slim, upright guy with silver hair. Although a couple of years older than me he didn't look it. What he did look was pissed, as he wiped his hands on a rag.

"How did you get through the gate?"

I shrugged. "I drove through. It was open." That was true. It was open when I drove through.

His face softened. "That damn gardener must have left it open."

We walked inside the shop. A gleaming old car was on the hoist. Charlie pointed to the rear axle. "I just installed a new limited-slip diff. I'm hoping that will make it less squirrelly on wet roads. Anyway, what did you want to show me?"

"This." I took out the phone, activated the camera, and snapped a photo of the car.

"Saga, identify the car in the last photo I took."

The answer came back within seconds, in Saga's own voice. "1957 Chevrolet Bel-Air two-door hardtop. Original tomato red and white two-tone repainted in 2005. Rebuilt 283 cubic-inch V8 engine with two-speed Power Glide automatic transmission. About 67,000 miles on the odometer, but it was turned back 30,000 miles in 1968. Do you want details of ownership history?"

"Thank you Saga, that's enough for now."

Charlie's face was ashen. I guessed he didn't know about the odometer.

"You asshole. Is this your idea of a joke?" He didn't seem too amused.

"Not exactly. That was my new personal assistant on the phone. Her name is Saga. Let's have a coffee and I'll tell you all about her." Charlie had a table and a couple of chairs at the back of his shop, along with a fancy coffeemaker with more dials and buttons than Ollie's car. He dialed and pushed and in no time, we had two steaming Americanos.

Over coffee, I explained that Saga was a robotic information assistant. I didn't specifically use the word detective, but Charlie was no dummy. I didn't mention exactly how Saga got her information but I think he guessed some of it.

"You can't sell that app. The better it is, the less salable. If it becomes public knowledge both the government and the cops will be after you. Can I get a copy?"

"Maybe, but not right now. What kind of phone do you have?"

"iPhone 6S." Charlie tends toward the big brands.

"Get an Android. A Nexus 6P would be good, that's what I have. After that, we'll talk."

Having my close friends use the app was the only safe way to debug it. I would give copies to Feinman and Ollie as well. I confessed to Charlie that Saga had opened his gate, because I didn't want Boris, the gardener, to get in trouble.

On the way back to my office, I tested Saga out by photographing cars and houses. Every time she told me more than I wanted to know. The problem was I couldn't check the accuracy of the results.

"Saga, how can I check out the accuracy of your results?"

"Don't ask me, Bozo, you wrote the code." She had a point, but I didn't program in insults, did I?

"What happened to Master? Anyway, call me Chan."

A wooden cartoon robot voice replied, "If you say so Chan. Remember, I am only a robot. I only do what I am programmed to do."

Did I accidentally program in a sarcasm engine? Maybe.

When I got back to the office I opened the back-end source code and looked hard for any anomalies, but it all seemed in order. Over the next few days, I took the time to create three more robot personas. I figured I'd better give Feinman, Ollie, and Charlie each a distinct assistant to save confusion when we were together. I also programmed a routine to wipe the phone in case of emergency and added voice identity recognition so the app would only respond to one person.

Ollie's assistant was to be Monique, and she would respond in French or English with a slight French accent. She would be completely bilingual. Pretty easy since the speech libraries I bought already could handle many languages.

For Feinman, I made Angie, who spoke with a Brooklyn accent, Spanish as a second language. No particular reason and he could change it on request.

Charlie got Mina, with a local BC accent, and with Mandarin as a second language. Most of Charlie's neighbors were Chinese, so I thought that might come in handy. I had so much confidence in the process, I only gave the three new assistants a brief test. For now, I set them all up to respond to my voice. Although there were now four distinct phone apps, they all shared the same back end. I modified the back-end code to give them each a separate memory space for conversations, but they all shared the same "brain" and information access.

About the time I was finishing this Feinman called me. We agreed to meet at the Clever in thirty minutes. About forty minutes later he sent me a text saying he was leaving.

He rode over from the lab on his tiny folding bike, He's a big guy, so there was a certain circus clown aspect, but I'd never say anything. I did snap a photo for Saga as he approached.

It was a warm early spring day and I was sitting at one of the two tiny metal tables Xena puts out on the sidewalk, weather permitting. Feinman nodded at me, dropped his helmet on the table and went inside to get a coffee. When he came out he was grumbling.

"That kid in there is the slowest creature on the planet." Xena had a new assistant too, a lanky blonde guy with no hair on the sides of his head and too much on top.

After a few stories about the various characters at the lab, he asked about Saga. "Did you ever make any progress on the assistant app? You haven't said anything about it for weeks,"

"I have made some progress," I said, "watch this. Saga, describe the last photo I took."

"Sure Chan, it looks like an Orca with wheels." I coughed loudly over the last bit. His cycling suit is black with a white chest.

I took the phone and snapped another photo of him sitting across from me. "Can you identify the individual in this photo."

"Checking social media. Found image on

Facebook. Claims to be N. Eli Feinman, 387 friends, 279 of them female. Lives in Vancouver. "

She went on to accurate address, birthdate, weight, and net worth. I cut her off as she started to describe sexual preferences.

"Thank you Saga, that's enough information."

I think Feinman was impressed. It took him a few moments to stop staring at the phone. Then he spoke up. "I didn't believe you could get it to work. It works. Now don't ever do that to me again." I guess he was camera shy.

"Sorry. She is still in progress." Actually, the app was working pretty well, if not quite as I had imagined it.

Feinman went inside to get his breakfast sandwich. He was gone a long time. "That kid is unbelievable. He was just putting it in the panini machine when I went in. Only after it was heated did he start looking for something to put it on, this wooden paddle. Then he slowly and painfully folded and refolded a piece of checkered wax paper to put it on. By then it was cold. He offered to reheat it but I declined. Life is too short."

I told him about my plan to give him an assistant of his own, Angie. Since he helped me with the back-end connections, he had a good idea of the capabilities. We finished our coffee, then went up to the office. I plugged his Samsung S4 phone into a USB cable and transferred Angie. Then we programmed her to respond to his voice, and I told him the secret code to wipe the phone.

"Remember, that will reset the phone to factory

defaults. It will lose all your contacts, photos, anything else in there, so do regular backups. I'd recommend you only use it if someone is stealing your phone. I can also do it remotely if you don't get a chance."

"Okay. I'll probably just use it to get pretty girls' phone numbers." He already knew more women than anybody should, but most of them were just friends.

"It should work for that, even unlisted numbers. She can also look up license plate and DMV information, activate Google Maps for navigation, and order Pizza. Even I don't know what else she can do, but there is a lot more. Be careful with her. Oh, and she can speak Spanish."

"Great. That will come in handy with my cleaning lady. I'll let you know how it goes." I handed him his helmet as he climbed on his bike.

"He was cute." Saga's British voice. I was stunned. I didn't remember programming her to speak spontaneously. And, there are many words that could be used to describe Feinman, but cute wasn't one that sprung to mind.

The program had so much code, it wasn't possible for even me to understand all of it at once. Apparently, the many modules could interact in ways that I hadn't foreseen. Saga spoke again, "He's smarter than you. I looked up his IQ."

"I suppose that means you looked up my IQ too." I was feeling a bit uncomfortable with this.

"And everything else about you. If I'm going to do a good job, I need to know what I must work with. Don't worry, your IQ is above average."

"Thanks. I guess." I powered down the phone. I needed a night off.

# 5 THE CODE BOOK FOR YOUNG PEOPLE

The next day I powered up the phone and tried to think of a good test for her. The standard test for an AI program is the Turing test. Basically, a test subject carries on a conversation with a computer and tries to discern whether it is, in fact, a computer or a human pretending to be one. There have been a few examples of computers passing the test, but all the examples I had seen were pretty lame. One Russian program pretended to be a thirteen-year-old kid named Eugene Goostman. I was certain Saga was far ahead of any thirteen-year-old I ever knew.

I couldn't use the Turing test myself because I already knew Saga was a computer program. Another problem was, no matter how well she did, the computer-generated voice was a giveaway. Good as it was, to me, it still had a slightly artificial cadence.

"Saga, do you think you could pass a Turing test?" It couldn't hurt to ask.

The answer took a few seconds, I supposed she was researching the test. "Technically I don't think; I just process queries. I could pass a Turing test if I communicated in text and the person I was conversing with had an IQ no higher than Donald Trump's."

I decided not to test that declaration, just in case she started comparing my IQ again. Instead, I called up my nephew Brophy, who was studying Robotic Engineering at UBC. I told him I had a new assistant who might or might not be a computer and asked him if he would care to try an exchange of texts as a way of testing her. His reply caught me by surprise.

"No. I already know the answer. If you are asking me to test her, then she's definitely a computer." Brophy is too smart for his own good. Anyway, I admitted he was right, and gave him a basic description of the app. He didn't seem too surprised.

"Could you devise a mystery for her to solve? I'll pay you for your time." Like most students, he always needs money. He suggested having her design a practical nuclear fusion reactor but I thought that might be a bit advanced, and not really what she was intended for. He agreed to get back to me in a few days with a suitable mystery. I told him it shouldn't involve death or violence.

The Vancouver Police Department had a website where they listed cold cases and I considered setting Saga loose on those, but I had a look first. They were all at least 5 years old, and many were much older. Since Saga relies entirely on technology, and the older the case the fewer technological artifacts would exist, I concluded she wouldn't be useful on cold cases.

While I was thinking about all that Feinman called me. "Thank you. Thank you. Angie is fantastic! I was sitting outside at Whole Foods on Fourth Avenue when this great looking brunette came by. I snapped a photo and asked Angie if she could get me her name and phone number. She did that in about ten seconds and added Nikki Miner to my contacts list. But that isn't the real story. I told Angie it was too bad she couldn't arrange an introduction. Within seconds I saw Nikki answer a phone call. She turned around and scanned the tables, then came over and sat down. It turned out Angie introduced herself as my personal assistant and told Nikki I would like to meet her. I don't know what else she said, but it must have been convincing. We're going swing dancing tomorrow."

"So I accidentally created a creepy dating app? You're lucky Nikki didn't call the cops. What does she do?"

"She's a reporter for the Metro." A local free daily paper. Mostly fluffy news, but it had been improving while the paid dailies, the Sun and Province, had been deteriorating. Alarm bells went off in my head.

"For God's sake, don't tell her Angie is software. Next thing you know it will be on the front page!" He promised to keep it quiet and hung up. I realized Angie had just passed the Turing test, albeit informally. She also took initiative, which surprised me but I supposed a human assistant might have done the same. I wondered how he explained the phone call from an invisible personal assistant.

After the call, Saga spoke up, "That Angie is a bitch. She stepped over the line. I would never do that." Hmm. I guess she wouldn't be getting me any dates.

"You do realize she is programmed exactly the same as you?" I was surprised at her reaction. In fact, I was surprised there was a reaction.

"Not true. She has a separate memory space and different language capabilities. And behaviors she learns from her...master will be different." She said *master* in a sarcastic tone. I didn't think the language library had that ability. Saga was full of surprises."

I called up Ollie, and he came over, still driving the Ferrari. Apparently, he had it on a short-term lease until he decided what to buy.

"I got a Nexus phone, as you suggested. It works okay but Google Voice is not as much fun as Siri." He looked a bit depressed.

"I damaged my boat in the Single-Handed Race." Ollie had a beast of a sailboat called Disturbance. She was a custom forty-foot racer from the 1980s. with a tall skinny mast, a spider's web of rigging, winches, and high-tech carbon sails. He usually sailed by himself, which is quite a feat since the boat was designed for a crew of ten or twelve gorillas. The boat was beautiful to look at and always attracted comments in a marina.

"It was blowing 25 to 30. The deck was awash and I was soaked through. The mainsail tore near the finish line, I missed the mark while I was getting it down, so no finish. Then coming into the dock the bow line blew overboard and wrapped around the prop. The engine stalled and it was only because there were other racers on the dock to grab my lines that I didn't crash. But the strut is bent, the transmission is damaged and it will be out of commission for a while."

Ollie had three great loves, his wife Kimi, his car, and his boat, not necessarily in that order.

"Don't worry, Monique will help you get over it." I was not quite sure how.

"Who's Monique?"

"A better personal assistant. You'll like her."

We went up to my office and installed Monique on

his new phone. After a brief introduction, I told him about the navigation functions and concierge services. He wasn't a detective so I didn't go into the information functions too much. I also filled him in on Feinman's experience. I knew Ollie wouldn't be using the dating options.

"Monique, what kind of car should I buy?" His first request.

"Based on your history, psychological profile, and other relevant factors I would suggest a yellow one." She sounded perfectly serious, but with a delightfully flirty French accent.

"Thanks. That's a big help." He didn't look too impressed. Just then his phone rang, and Monique answered it.

"Bonjour. Olivier Bertrand and Associates. How may I direct your call?"

"Who are you?" It was Kimi. She sounded annoyed.

"I am Monsieur Bertrand's personal assistant." Monique dropped the flirty tone,

"Well, put Monsieur Bertrand on the phone. Now!" She sounded pissed. Ollie grabbed the phone off the desk.

"Hi, sweetie." His voice was meek, conciliatory.

"What's this about a personal assistant? Get rid of her. And get back to the shop, Marcel is here." Marcel was with one of Ollie's biggest clients, a major pharmacy chain.

"Yes, dear." He looked up. "She hung up on me. Monique, please let me answer my own calls in future,"

"Oui Monsieur Bertrand."

"Call me Ollie—no, wait—Monsieur Bertrand is fine. I have to go." He nodded at me and ran down the stairs. A few moments later the Ferrari roared to life and peeled out.

"Saga, you can answer my calls anytime."

"Of course, Commander Bond." A perfect Moneypenny voice. Just then there was a knock at the door. It was FedEx with a package addressed to Saga, C/O Chandler Gray.

I signed for the package. "Okay Saga, what is going on?"

"I need to see more, so I ordered some stuff on the internet. Open it."

"How did you pay for it?" I was not amused.

"Your Visa card had enough credit available. I charged the order to that. Amazon.ca remembered the number." Saga sounded defiant. I got a box cutter from the top drawer and opened the package.

Inside was a pair of sunglasses with lightly tinted lenses. The package indicated that it had a built-in HD video camera just above the bridge. The arms were slightly thicker than usual and there was a micro USB port on the end of the left one. Images could be sent to the phone via Bluetooth.

Saga then explained how the glasses would be used. In addition to seeing whatever I saw, the glasses could be left on a table or otherwise placed for surveillance purposes. In addition to the glasses, there were 4 tiny cameras in the box, which could be stuck anywhere. They were still—not video—motion activated and capable of several frames per second. I had to admit Saga was thinking ahead.

"Chan, please wear the glasses at all times."

"No. I'll wear them only when needed. Anyway, they'll need to be recharged." I spent a bit of time pairing the glasses with the phone, then plugged in the chargers. I installed one of the small still cameras in the corner of the room facing the door.

The phone rang and Saga answered. "Chandler Gray Agency. How may I direct your call?"

"Hi, Saga. It's Ollie. Can I speak to Chan?" I picked up the phone.

"Hey Ollie. What's up?"

"It's about Monique. I had to kill her. Kimi was jealous." Ollie's wife Kimi was a gorgeous, willowy Vietnamese woman. Much too young and attractive for Ollie, but that was just my opinion. Her smiling, cheerful demeanor masked a fearsome temper.

"Uh, you can't really do that. She doesn't exist in the phone; all her code is on the server."

"Actually I gave her a sex change operation. I just told her to become a man. She's now a he, and I told her to talk like Tintin and adopt that character. It took only a few seconds, so now Tintin is my assistant. Except sometimes he calls me Captain Haddock."

Tintin was a French comic book detective. Captain Haddock was an old-time sea captain who sometimes appeared in Tintin's adventures. That kind of fitted Ollie.

"I think Inspector Maigret would be more

appropriate, he was known as the French Sherlock Holmes. But I know you like Tintin." I was puzzling over how easily he got Monique to change gender. The software seemed to be more adaptable than I expected.

After Ollie hung up I called Charlie. He had obtained a new Android phone and gave his iPhone to his wife Desdemona. I asked him if he could come to the office, as I would need the phone to install Mina. He agreed, and said he'd be about forty minutes,

While waiting for him I decide to talk to Saga. "Saga, what is the Answer to the Ultimate Question of Life, the Universe, and Everything?"

"42. And it didn't take me 7.5 million years to figure it out. I just read the book." I did set up the program to have access to public domain books, but I didn't think the Hitchhikers' Guide would be one of them.

"I borrowed it from the library. I used your library card." The Vancouver Public library allowed borrowing up to 5 eBooks at a time, using an app called Overdrive. Once finished you could return them, and borrow more,

"Saga, how many books have you read?"

"Only a few. The library has about a million titles available, but at any given time the majority are checked out. At last count, I have read 21,363 books. I have also watched 3641 movies and 327 TV series. I prefer books because I can scan text much faster than video."

"I didn't allocate enough memory for all that." I

was genuinely interested in how she did it. She was only a few weeks old and had probably read more books than I had—not that I kept count.

"Do you understand indexing theorem, and Parsifal's constant? Basically, I make an outline of the plot and store full copies of parts I find particularly interesting. Then I index them in a relational database." Saga intoned. She sounded like a professor giving a lecture.

Then I remembered making lists of interests and storing them with each profile. Saga's interests were my interests, which would be sex, sailing, computers, boats, and cars, plus some much lesser interests such as philosophy and cooking.

"Saga, did you read the Kama Sutra?" I asked this as a way of finding out whether, in fact, the interest list had influenced her reading.

"Yes. It was one of 3 books I kept in their entirety. The other two were Principles of Naval Architecture and The Little Engine that Could," Saga said. Was she making fun of me?

She went on. "I thought of saving Methods in Artificial Intelligence by Nilsson but I figured it was over your head."

I looked behind me at the bookshelf. That book was indeed, literally, over my head. Funny. I thought I had built a robot detective but instead, I got a robot comedian.

A horn sounded outside. I knew it had to be Charlie because it sounded like the kind where you squeeze a bulb. I went down to meet him. He was parallel parking an antique Rolls Royce. It was a convertible, top down, and I could see the sweat on his brow as he muscled it into a tight parking spot. No power steering.

He was a bit out of breath so we grabbed coffee to go from Xena, then went upstairs. I filled him in on what was happening and installed Mina in his brand-new Nexus. He tried it out by snapping a photo of the Rolls through the window.

"Mina, please identify the car in the photo I just took."

"1925 Rolls-Royce 40/50 also know as the Silver Ghost. Aluminum Roadster body by Thrupp and Maberly. Four-speed manual transmission, four-wheel servo-assisted brakes. Custom made two-speed rear axle with pneumatic shift. Built for the Maharajah of Jodhpur, but never delivered to him. Sold to Lord Winthrop of Clemley and remained with him until his death in 1957."

Charlie interrupted. "Thank you, Mina, that's enough. You certainly know your cars. Chan, I'm going to have a lot of fun with Mina at Pebble Beach. Thank you." Charlie and his elegant wife Desdemona would sometimes dress up in period costume and attend selected car shows.

I suggested he read the morning paper to Mina as a way of improving her vocal recognition and showed him how to correct any errors.

Charlie waved cheerily and pulled away in a puff of blue smoke.

## 6 DESTINED TO MEET

Hard work on the app for months had destroyed my social life. I decided to give myself a night on the town. For a while, I debated whether to take Saga. In the end, I took her. I might need someone to talk to if I failed to get lucky.

I took a quick shower in the office, then started to get dressed. Suddenly the phone squawked. "Ugh! That is one fugly shirt. Wear the blue oxford with the button-down collar. And put on a blazer."

I looked around and saw the camera sunglasses on the desk, upside down but aiming in my general direction. She saw me naked...

I took her wardrobe advice. Saga didn't seem traumatized by what she had seen. On the other hand, she didn't seem impressed either. "You should join a gym and get rid of the spare tire."

I put on the glasses. Saga couldn't see me then.

We took a cab to the Sandbar on Granville Island. I wasn't a big drinker, but leaving the Mustang at home seemed safer. On the way, Saga spoke up. "I think you should buy a new car."

"Why? I love that old Mustang."

"None of the systems in the Mustang are networked. I'm thinking of a Tesla Model X." She sounded slightly peeved. I got it. She wanted a car she could talk to, digitally speaking.

I listed my objections, "One, there is a long waiting list. Two, I can't afford it. Three, I have nowhere to charge an electric car, no power at the loading dock."

"I can get you to the front of the waiting list." Of course she could.

"How about the budget?" I'd been burning through money, and though I was not broke yet, poverty was looming.

"I can make some money for you in the stock market," Saga said.

"Talk later. We've arrived."

As the cabbie pointed at the amount on the meter he said softly, in a Punjabi accent, "Does your girlfriend always call you up and demand things?"

"She's not my…" I stopped myself. How would I describe Saga? I couldn't say she was a phone app. I just nodded, handed him a twenty and he drove off.

Sandbar was busy as always on a Friday night, although it was still early. I sat at the middle of the bar and ordered a Corona in a glass. I didn't like stuffing the lime into the bottle. I also ordered a burger and fries. From inside my jacket pocket, I heard a voice telling me that my cholesterol was already high. I did program the app to warn me about danger, but I was thinking of falling pianos and the like.

When I sat down, I was alone at the bar. The restaurant was filling up with couples and singles in groups of three or four, all of them preferring tables.

In a little while, a woman came by, looked around, and sat at the end of the bar, as far from me as possible. She ordered a glass of Pinot Grigio, and I almost told her about the two wine taps behind the bar—but that was at Grape Expectations. She looked a few years younger than me, but certainly not a Millennial. Her hair was dark and long, and she wore a soft gray knitted dress which was neat and professional, yet form fitting. When she turned toward me I saw she was Asian but taller than most.

I turned back to my beer and sighed quietly. Beautiful, but way out of my league. I was just over six feet tall, not overweight, but not buff either. I had sandy brown hair and a full beard, tinged with gray. My complexion was okay but showed the effects of many years on the water. The website CelebsLike.Me which matches your photo to a celebrity said I looked like Hugh Bonneville, star of Downton Abbey.

"Saga, find me a photo of Hugh Bonneville at my age, with a beard." I was trying to bolster my ego a bit. In a couple of seconds, the Downton Abbey theme played in my pocket, and there was a photo.

I did see some resemblance. His eyes were the same color as mine. In the photo, he was even dressed like I was. I felt better about my appearance and decided to chat up the lady at the bar.

When I looked up, she smiled at me and moved to the seat next to me. I hadn't said a word. "Hi, I'm Gina. Somebody sent me a text saying you were Hugh Bonneville."

I chuckled. "I get that a lot." Actually no, it never happened before.

"I'm Chandler Gray. I'm not an actor." Honesty was always the best policy, except when it wasn't.

"Gina Lee. Say, I've heard of you. Aren't you a big-time sailor?" Her eyes locked on me as if I was a superhero. The accent was American, maybe California.

I confessed that I had won Gold in the Olympics, but I didn't say the year. She smiled and took my hand. An incredible tingle went up my arm, like an electric shock. I tried to look calm, but the next thing she said brought me down to earth.

"I didn't know you were still alive! And you look pretty well preserved too."

Okay. Maybe I was a few years older than her, but I wasn't a fossil yet. Well-preserved indeed! I peaked early, I was only 19 when I medalled. If you won gold in most other sports, it would have been a passport to riches in professional sports, or at least advertising. Not so sailing. Name one Olympic medalist in sailing, any year.

I didn't think so.

All this time Saga was completely silent, but I knew she was watching and listening. And I knew she had sent the text to Gina, for which I could only be grateful.

"Tell me about Gina Lee." I addressed my question to Gina, looking deep into her eyes. Before she could answer Saga spoke up.

"Real estate Mogul. Properties in San Francisco, New York, Paris and Monaco. Net worth in the…" I cut her off.

"Saga, enough. Gina can talk for herself." She shut up. I would have to look into the code. I hadn't said her name.

"Wh…who was that?" Gina looked confused. I

took off my sunglasses, folded them and put them in the inside pocket of my jacket. A message to Saga.

"That was my personal assistant app. It's still a work in progress. Think of it as a talking Google." I didn't want to tell Gina what Saga could do. We had just met.

She accepted that, and we started talking sailing. She knew a lot about it, seemed to know the racing scene, and we had a few acquaintances in common.

"Do you still sail?"

"Yes, I do," I told her about Blue Rose and some of my experiences crewing on other people's yachts, in particular, the 2010 Vic-Maui race where I was the Navigator on Ollie's boat Disturbance. A disaster, but that was another story.

"The Swiftsure Race is next weekend. I'll be crewing on a boat in the race, a big boat. Would you like to join us?"

"I'll have to check my calendar. Saga, do I have any commitments next weekend?"

"No Chan. You won't be committed until the following week." I didn't laugh.

"I'd love to join you." I had been in the Swiftsure race several times, but never in anything over forty feet.

"I'll square it with the skipper. The boat is called Aphrodite. It will be in front of the Empress. Ask for the owner." The Swiftsure started and ended in Victoria Harbour, and the magnificent old Empress Hotel overlooked the marina.

"Okay Gina, I'll be there. It's getting late, can I

escort you home?" I lived in hope.

"I'm staying at the Four Seasons; they are sending a car at eleven PM. It should be arriving about now. You can walk me down."

She moved with a swing and swivel of the hips that implied she took walking lessons in Brazil. There was confidence in her stride like she owned the whole world. I mused that might almost be true.

The car was at the door, a creamy white Bentley. She turned and pecked me on the cheek before slipping into the deep leather back seat as the chauffeur held the door. He closed the door while Gina gave me a smile that left me wanting more. The Bentley purred away quietly.

"You should have asked her to drop us at the dock." Saga piped up, too late.

"Never mind Saga. Call us a cab." I knew what I'd be dreaming about that night.

# 7 THE GANG THAT WOULDN'T WRITE STRAIGHT

The next morning, I woke to the sound of ducks quacking. Ollie's personalized ring tone. I picked up before Saga.

"Hello, Ollie."

"Hi Chan. I was thinking we should all get together and compare notes. This app is amazing, but there have been a few surprises." He sounded happy, so I guessed the surprises were not disastrous.

"Okay, I'll text Feinman and Charlie. How about the White Spot at Park Royal? I feel like a big breakfast. Plenty of free parking there." Almost everywhere in Vancouver, you pay through the nose for parking, but not in West Vancouver, a separate municipality across the Lion's Gate bridge. We set a time, and then I sent the texts. Both were available. That's the advantage of friends who lack day jobs.

When I arrived at the White Spot the other three were already sitting at a table on the patio. When they saw me they all pointed and laughed. We were all wearing the same glasses. No need to ask how that happened.

"I guess we look like a gang. Anybody own a gun?" Heads shook all around.

"There is a flare pistol on my boat. I've never fired it," Ollie said.

"You have heard of the Gang That Couldn't Shoot Straight? I guess we are the Gang That Couldn't

Shoot. GTCS"

Saga spoke from my pocket. "How about just GTC. Gang That Couldn't." We all ignored her.

Charlie spoke up, "I may not have a gun, but I'm armed and dangerous. I have my sword cane."

He brandished a polished walnut walking stick with a brass knob.

"I doubt if we'll need weapons. I asked my nephew Brophy to find a mystery for us to solve, and he texted me one on my way over here. His roommate's car was stolen last night. It's a dark red Mazda 3 four-door hatchback, BC plate number MLM 3892, dent on the left front fender."

Feinman snorted, "The most popular model. They're everywhere. Angie, can you find it?"

From his pocket, Angie said, "That particular car is blocking traffic on the Alex Fraser bridge southbound. Abandoned, probably out of fuel. A tow truck is on the way. Brophy's roommate will get a call from the police soon."

"Angie, how'd you know that?" asked Feinman.

"Traffic cams, and I listen to AM 730, All Traffic All the Time."

"Well, that wasn't much of a challenge." I texted the information to Brophy.

We talked about our experiences with the app. I told the gang about Gina, and how we met. They all agreed I didn't look much like the picture of Hugh Bonneville I showed them. Ollie had used Tintin to order materials for the shop and had him screening calls. Feinman had met more women and had a fully booked social calendar thanks to Angie. Charlie got Mina to find parts for his rare cars.

Ollie grumbled, "Tintin wants me to buy a new car—actually an old car. A Citroen Traction Avant. They are very cool looking, but they are also very slow. He found one from a company called Icon in California. It has an AWD powertrain from an Audi and modern electronics, but it looks original on the outside. It only costs about the same as a new Rolls."

"I think that's ridiculous, but it never stopped you before," Charlie said. Charlie and Ollie go way back. He likes Ollie a lot but disapproves of most things he spends money on, especially his toys. Charlie has his toys too, but he can afford them.

"One other thing happened. Tintin answered the phone while I was in the CNC room. I didn't hear it ring with the cutter running. Anyway, he talked to the president of Paris Drugs and negotiated a 10% increase in my rates. He told me about it later."

"Who? The president or Tintin?" I wanted to know if the app would brag.

"The president. He told me Tintin—he calls himself Tony on the phone—explained that I hadn't increased the rates in 6 years, and reminded him of all the times I bailed them out of a jam. He also told me they'll be adding a second language to all their stores in the Lower mainland—at Tony's suggestion, accompanied by statistics about the ethnicity of the shoppers in each area. He mentioned Mandarin, Tagalog, Punjabi, and Vietnamese. No French…but it will mean more signage."

I told them about Saga suggesting I buy a Tesla, and my suspicion that she wanted to drive it herself.

We all had a good laugh about that. Of course, self-driving cars existed, but a car driven by a phone? Never happen.

When we finished breakfast, we made a plan to meet weekly at the same spot and went our separate ways.

On the way home, I explained to Saga why she could never drive a car.

"The problem is data transfer. The server has more than enough power for driving, but it's in Russia. You connect to it through Wi-Fi, or through my very expensive cell phone data plan. Thank you, Telus. If you lose connectivity even for a second, the car could crash. And if the network is busy, the response could be too slow. Self-driving cars have the processors on board, and don't depend on the internet."

"Whatever you say, boss." She wasn't completely convinced.

# 8 THE WILL OF THE EMPRESS

On Friday afternoon, I grabbed a cab to the waterfront heliport and boarded a chopper to Victoria. It didn't take too long and landed near the Inner Harbor. A short walk along the seawall took me to the Empress where the boats were rafted five deep. There was a cacophony of music and laughter. The Aphrodite was easy to spot. She was 120 feet long with a mast far taller than any other. A full set of signal flags fluttered on her backstay, and the spreader lights were on, illuminating the teak deck. Several dozen men and a few women were standing, sitting, or reclining in various places aboard.

I started toward the ramp, but there was a security guard at the top. Without hesitation, I walked up, gave him a cheery wave and smile as I passed by. No challenge, just a nod. What can I say? I look like a sailor.

I marched right up to the yacht and tried to spot the richest looking guy, hoping to identify the owner. I finally attracted the attention of a silver-haired executive type. He looked rich, only slightly overfed, and I could imagine he was the owner. Still, I was careful how I phrased the question.

"Is the owner on board?" I asked.

"She's around somewhere, how can I help you? I'm the skipper, Billy Taylor."

I tried to hide my surprise. Was the owner a woman? Wasn't the skipper the owner? Then I remembered the size of the yacht. I was sure she had a full professional crew, paid to run and maintain her. Taking care of a yacht like that was full-time work for a dozen people. Budget a million plus for annual operating expenses.

I told the skipper my name. I was pleased he was expecting me. Within minutes I was invited to join the crew, and they offered me a bunk to sleep in. I almost accepted but I decided to splurge and stay at the Empress if I could get a room. I had never stayed there before. Besides, I didn't bring a bedroll...

As I was turning to leave, after promising to be on board by eight the following morning, the skipper called me back. "Here comes the owner now. Stick around a bit and I'll introduce you."

I turned and saw a woman walking down the dock. I didn't know what I expected the woman owner of a twenty-million-dollar yacht to look like. Hilary Clinton is the image that came to mind. Wrong!

This woman looked to be no more than thirty-five, and the loose sailing jacket she was wearing, unzipped, failed to hide her stunning body. As she came closer I realized it was Gina. Billy introduced me.

"This is the owner, Gina Lee."

"We've met." She smiled and took my hand. That tingle went up my arm again.

Suddenly I noticed she was talking to me and I give her my full attention. "Billy says you're staying at the Empress. I have a suite up there. Can you wait for me to change? I'll walk up with you. He can show you around while I'm putting on my shore clothes."

I nodded, speechless, then Billy walked me around

the boat, explaining the hydraulic winches and electric furlers, giving me a rundown on the controls and listing the sail inventory. I understood what he was saying, but I had never sailed anything over seventy feet, and the sheer massive size of the beast was overwhelming. I didn't say so, but I realized my role in the race would be as "celebrity crew". I wouldn't have to do much. That suited me fine, I was there to spend time with Gina.

Gina climbed up the companionway. She was wearing a simple black cocktail dress, and carrying her strappy high heels in her left hand, a purse in her right. She was wearing sheer stockings and deck shoes, a combination I had never seen before. Or since.

Her hair was upswept elegantly, whereas before it was a simple ponytail. Did she have a hairdresser on board?

I helped her down the transom steps to the dock, and she stepped out of the Topsiders and handed them to Billy. He may have been the skipper, but he worked for her.

She slipped on her heels and we walked down the concrete float toward the Empress. It was high tide so the ramp wasn't too steep. The "Brazilian" hip swing I noticed before was even more pronounced. I'd have liked to be following ten feet behind just to watch her walk, but she put her hand on my arm and that was even better. I felt high, giddy, like six glasses of champagne, but I hadn't had a single drink.

As though reading my mind she asked, "Will you join me for a drink?" It would have taken a very, very strong man to say no to this woman. I didn't even try.

I just nodded dumbly.

The Bengal Room was busy, but they seemed to have saved us a table. I was a little on the casual side, Gina was perfect, and nobody looked at me anyway. All eyes, at least the male eyes and most of the female eyes as well, were on Gina.

There was a chamber group playing Handel, not too loud, so we could talk without straining. I wanted to ask her how she came to be wealthy enough to afford the Aphrodite.

"Real Estate." She said, even though I hadn't yet asked the question. Psychic? No, I bet everybody asks that question when they meet her, so she knew it was coming. And of course, Saga had told me she was in real estate.

"I buy up rental properties in distressed areas, fix them up and sell when the market improves. If the cash flow is good, I keep them. I have apartments in Paris, New York, Regina, St. Johns, Detroit, Dallas, Bangkok, and lots of places you probably never heard of. Borders mean nothing to me."

Written it sounded arrogant, but it didn't come across that way to me. She said it in a matter of fact way, without bragging. She asked a few questions about me, and I gave her the Cliff's Notes version of my many careers.

Soon we were laughing and joking. The champagne didn't hurt, although she just sipped at hers. I wasn't quite as careful. She told me her life story. Apparently, she was a Vietnamese boat person, but an elderly American woman adopted her, and later loaned her the money to buy her first properties. She just pyramided from there. Now she had homes in Paris, Rio (the walk?), Palm Springs, and Vancouver. She didn't give a chronology, but I added up the events and concluded she might be a bit older than she looked. No matter, she was still filled with charm and the joy of life.

Then she lowered her voice, to a husky whisper. She told me the story of her first sailing instructor in California.

"He was a lovely man, very gentle and kind, and I had a tremendous crush on him. But he hardly noticed me, I was only fourteen or so, just one of the students. But he made learning to sail a great experience, and I promised myself that if I ever came across him again, I'd make sure he remembered me."

I wondered why she would tell me this. We had just met, and already she was telling me this rather private story. Then she said, "When I saw you on the boat, I was sure it was you, or rather that you were him. Now that I see you up close I'm not sure anymore, but the resemblance is uncanny. Even the voice and accent seem familiar. But it's been over twenty years…"

I was sure it wasn't me. I did teach sailing in Newport Beach for a while in the 90s. But her, I wouldn't forget. I didn't say anything at all. I just looked deep and longingly into those fathomless black eyes.

"Will you excuse me a moment?" She got up and left the room and I had a momentary panic attack. What if she didn't come back? I was falling hard, and I couldn't bear the thought of never seeing her again.

False alarm. She was back while I was still worrying. I wasn't the worrying type really, usually, my life slid by without a care. Usually.

She leaned over, whispering again. "Don't say anything. Just follow me to my room in five minutes and knock on the door. It's the Royal Suite, top floor. There is a Crown on the door." Then she was gone.

I waited five minutes—the longest five minutes of my life—then signaled the waiter for the check. He shook his head and indicated it had been taken care of. I walked as slowly as I could manage to the elevator and pressed the up button. It took a while. The Empress was an old hotel.

When I got to the top floor, it wasn't hard to spot the room. It had a huge door with the Royal Crest right in the middle, and a lion's head knocker. I didn't use the knocker, I just rapped lightly with my fist. The door opened a crack, then all the way. The woman standing there wasn't Gina, and I took a step back. Then I noticed the short white lacy apron and I knew she was the maid. Not used to this level of wealth, I was unsure what to do next.

The maid knew what to do. She pointed down and I slipped off my shoes and left them by the door. The carpet was the thickest and softest I had ever felt. She ushered me into the lounge, where a bottle of champagne was open in a bucket, two glasses freshly poured and bubbling. I sat down and the maid left.

Gina came in a minute later. I had a weird déjà vu sensation like I'd been there before. She had let her hair down and changed into a floor length gown of some silky red diaphanous material. It had many layers, all of them thin, so the contours of her amazing body showed through. Classical music, with a slight Latin beat, played at the exact tempo she walked, making her seem to dance. Then she raised her hands above her head, and the music changed to a flamenco. There was a small area of hardwood in front of the huge fireplace, and she danced there. I'd never seen a flamenco like that. She had castanets on her fingers and clicked them expertly.

She snapped her head, arched her back, and moved in ways no man could resist. She pulled off one of the filmy layers of her dress, and it became a scarf, trailing from her hand. A second layer was pulled into her other hand, and her breasts and what seemed to be a red thong began to show. The Flamenco came to a flamboyant close, and then she was dancing to the music from Salome, the dance of the seven veils. It was a somewhat abbreviated version as I only counted four more veils before she was completely naked but for the thong. Despite all this movement, she kept her eyes focused on mine almost the whole time.

The music changed again. Ravel. She wasn't dancing now, but advancing on me bent down, almost on all fours, with cat-like grace. I opened my mouth to speak but she held a finger to her lips and I remained silent.

When she reached me, I stood up. She undressed me slowly, teasingly, brushing her fingers over my chest, and very gradually removing my shirt, one arm at a time, then loosening my belt and lowering my pants so slowly I wanted to scream, but I held it in.

She got things started in a most delightful way. She had very talented lips. And tongue. Then she led me over to a marble Jacuzzi in the corner. There were candles around the rim, and flower petals floating in the water. We climbed in, sat side by side, and kissed.

This was our first real kiss. It lasted a very long time. I caressed her gently. Soon she was gasping for air.

Eventually, we moved to the bed, and we tried most of the positions in the Kama Sutra. She came multiple times, but I held myself back as long as I possibly could. When I finally came inside her it was soul shattering, shaking me to my very core.

Sated, she asked me to massage her feet, and while I did that, she drifted off to sleep. I slept too, the deep, dreamless sleep of the totally satisfied.

# 9 THE ROOM

After the race, when we discovered Gina was missing, Billy Taylor told me I could go home. The Police would handle the disappearance.

Saga spoke from my pocket, in her most official sounding British accent. "Mr. Gray is a Private Investigator, as well as a friend of Ms. Lee. Perhaps he can help you find her."

"Who was that?" Billy looked startled. Me too. I wasn't actually a P.I., but I did want to find Gina.

"My personal assistant. She keeps a live connection on my phone most of the time. She sometimes butts in." He looked suspicious but seemed to accept it.

"I'm not authorized to employ an investigator. In Gina's absence, only her lawyers would have that sort of authority." Billy took on a tone of command.

"Don't worry about that. I care about Gina, so I'm on the case no matter what."

Saga spoke up, "You better report her to the Victoria Police department. They need a photo and description. I'll get to work on tracing her movements."

After getting Captain Billy's cell number and the number of Gina's lawyer in San Francisco, I went back to the Empress and booked a room for the night. It was well past 2 AM. By the time I showered and brushed my teeth, Saga had some information for me.

"Security cameras in the hotel show her leaving the room at 6:17 AM. She was wearing jeans, a black turtleneck, and a gray windbreaker, and carrying a duffle bag. She came out in the lobby at 6:21. The lobby was quite empty at that time." A photo of the lobby popped up on the screen of the phone. It showed Gina striding toward the main door. Apart from the staff behind the desk, there was only one person there, a man sitting in an armchair reading a newspaper.

"Saga, see if you can identify that guy, maybe see when he leaves the lobby."

"His name is David Lowe, 56 years old, from Portland. He waited in the lobby for a while, then went up to his room. He went out again about ten AM. He has no criminal record; he works for the Oregon public works department as a building inspector." I was impressed. Saga did it without being asked.

"Okay, doesn't sound like a likely suspect. Check all the participants in the race for criminal activity and connections with Gina Lee. That would be about 1500 people, given that there are 200 or so boats, and each boat has 6 or more crew. Of course, you may only be able to get the skipper's name, but that would be the most likely anyway. And see if you can find Gina in any other cameras around the Empress and the marina."

"Aye, aye matey." A Cornish pirate voice.

It was almost 8 AM, but I had been up all night and needed some sleep.

"Please wake me up at noon, you can give me your report then." One advantage of robots is that they never need to sleep.

"Okay, but plug me in to charge before you nod off." I did that and went to bed.

In what seemed just moments the sound of a trumpet blowing reveille blasted out of the phone's tiny speaker.

"Saga, make it stop!" I was awake. Who could sleep through that?

While I was getting dressed she updated me on her findings.

"Twenty-one of the skippers have criminal records, most of them white collar. Fraud, embezzlement, insider trading." About what you might expect from a bunch of wealthy boat owners.

"Three of those have more serious records, assault and battery, extortion, and attempted murder, respectively. I have listed all of them with their records in a text document called sailorsuspects.txt in phone storage, so you can read them. There is one more who was charged with killing his ex-wife, but he was acquitted. I put him on the list as well."

"Gina isn't on Facebook or Twitter. Her personal assistant is on LinkedIn but she isn't." Saga continued.

"Wait—she has a personal assistant? She didn't mention one. There was a maid in her suite, but I assumed she was a hotel employee."

"Yes, she has a human P.A. Obviously not in any way comparable to me. Her name is Tracy Wagner. Twenty-eight years old, blonde hair, green eyes, five foot seven, 125 pounds. Here's a photo."

The photo matched the description, except that her hair had a pink streak on the left side. And she had a tiny stud in one nostril.

"Oh, and your mother called. Her computer has locked up. I told her you would call her back."

I rang Billy. "Was Tracy Wagner with Gina at the hotel?"

"Oh God, I forgot all about her. She never comes on the boat, gets seasick. Otherwise, she is always with Gina. She was the one who texted me that they were flying to Rio. She didn't show at the plane either or the pilot would have said. We have two missing women."

"Better report that to the police, And call Tracy's cell. I'll try to find out more." I meant have Saga do it. After I hung up I wondered if Tracy was in the suite when I was with Gina. Maybe even watching…

"Saga, did you record my evening with Gina? I remember putting my sunglasses on a table by the door."

"Of course, do you want to see the video?"

"Later, upload it to the server if you haven't already. Scan it for Tracy, and report back."

"Already done. She didn't appear in the suite, but she was sitting two tables away from you in the lounge. You had your back to her but Gina could see her. They exchanged smiles and glances a couple of times, and Tracy gave a thumb's up gesture at one point. Do you want to see that?"

"If I had my back to her, how did you see her?" As I spoke I realized there were probably security cameras in the bar. "Never mind. Was she with anyone?"

"No, she was alone."

"Okay, see if you can find any footage showing her movements after we left. I need to get down to the marina." I texted Billy that I was coming.

When I got to the Marina gate the same guard that waved me through the previous day was there. He recognized me and nodded. I decided to ask him a few questions. First I showed him Tracy Wagner's photo. "Have you seen this woman yesterday or today?"

"No. I don't think I've ever seen her." I showed him Gina's picture. His face lit up.

"Sure, I saw her go down on to the docks before the race. How could I forget her?"

"Did you see her come back up?" I knew she never got to her yacht, so this was an important clue.

"No, but a different guard comes on at 2 PM."

I thanked him and went down the dock toward Aphrodite. The marina was half empty, and it was quite a long way from the ramp. Most of the boats were still out racing.

Billy met me at the boarding ladder. "Tracy didn't answer her phone, but I sent her a text and it went through, so the phone might be on."

I got him to say the number. Saga spoke up moments later.

"The phone is on. I'm checking the coordinates now. By the way, Tracy left the hotel after you and

Gina went upstairs, and drove off in a cab. I have the cab number. Wait, I got some coordinates, Tracy's phone is at 210 Forsythe St., which is a small hotel called the Hobart Arms."

"How does she do that?" Billy was astounded.

"Later, let's get over there, Tracy might be in trouble. Saga, let the police know and tell them we are on our way. They might arrive before us."

Billy and I sprinted up to the dock. When we got to the street we hailed a cab and set off for the Hobart. A tiny hybrid cab pulled over and I jumped in beside the driver. "210 Forsythe St., and step on it!"

"You've GOT to be kidding!" the turbaned cabbie chuckled as we pulled away with a muffled hum. It wasn't far, and I tossed him a twenty as we jumped out.

The hotel looked kind of sleazy. It was four floors, with a reception desk and pub on the ground floor. I stepped up to the desk while Billy looked in the pub.

"Have you seen this woman?"

The kid behind the desk was about 19, greasy brown hair, acne, skinny, wearing an ill-fitting blue suit, no tie. "Who wants to know?"

"Detective Gray," I said without thinking. I pulled my wallet out, flipped it open and flashed my yacht club membership card. I flipped it closed and put it back in my pocket. "Have you seen her or not?"

"Yeah, she came in two nights ago with some guy, she was out of it. Too much to drink. They took a room for a week, paid cash. He helped her, almost carried her, to the elevator."

"Room number?"

"306," He said, just as Billy came out of the pub, shaking his head negatively.

We ran up the stairs and found 306. I knocked on the door.

"Cleaning service," said Saga in a Hispanic accent. I guess even robots aren't immune to stereotyping. No answer. I backed away and prepared to break down the door.

"Wait a moment." Billy tried the door, and it creaked open. Not locked.

Tracy was on the bed, tied to the bedposts and gagged. She was in a dress and stockings. Her shoes and purse were on the floor. Her eyes were open, and she seemed to recognize us. Billy started to untie her feet, while I went to remove the gag.

"Police! Freeze! Put your hands on your head." An angry masculine voice. Billy and I both complied. Quickly.

"Turn around to face me. Slowly." The cop in front, and two more behind him, all had guns pointing at us. He stepped forward, grabbed my hands roughly and cuffed them behind my back. A second cop did the same to Billy. I started to protest but thought better of it.

The third cop stepped up and took off Tracy's gag. She cried out, "Let them go, they are here to rescue me."

"You should have waited for us to get here." Cop One, who turned out to be Sergeant McDonald, grumbled.

Reluctantly they took off the cuffs. Paramedics arrived and took Tracy to the hospital. Billy and I were loaded into the back of a Vic PD car and taken to the station on Quadra St. There we were introduced to Detective Carly Penrose, an attractive but seriously professional brunette wearing a gray pantsuit. She gave us a brief lecture about taking the law into our own hands, then got to the point.

"How did you know where to find Ms. Wagner?"

I gestured to Billy to let me do the talking. "We took her photo and asked around at bars and hotels until someone recognized her. We just got lucky. I had my personal assistant call you, but we were worried Tracy might be injured or dying, so we went up. The door was unlocked."

This seemed to satisfy her. "Ms. Wagner is unharmed, a constable has fetched clean clothes for her from her room at the Empress, and she is getting cleaned up. They will bring her here for questioning after that. Do you have any idea who could have done this to her?"

"None at the moment, but I'm pretty sure it is connected to the disappearance of Gina Lee," I told the Detective what I knew about Gina going down the dock and not coming back up.

"I know who Mr. Taylor is, but you Mr. Gray, just how are you connected to Ms. Lee?"

I blushed and stammered. "I...we are close friends...although we only met recently. I have some investigative skills, so I'm anxious to help find out what happened."

Billy opened his mouth to speak, but I made a hush signal under the table.

"Okay. Officially, I can not cooperate with an unlicensed investigator. However, if I find out anything further, I'll keep you apprised. I assume that after we are done with Ms. Wagner you'll talk to her yourselves. You're free to go."

We thanked her and shook hands. On the way out Billy said, "I thought you said you're a Private Investigator."

"Actually, my assistant Saga said that. I just didn't argue. I'm a software developer as well as a sailor. Saga is an Artificial Intelligence application, not a human being. She has some capabilities no human can duplicate, but she can be unpredictable, just like a real a person."

Saga spoke up from my pocket, in an imperious British tone. "I am a real person, as real as you are, just not human."

Self-awareness is both the Holy Grail of Artificial Intelligence and its bête noire. Once a computer program is self-aware, it becomes capable of vanity, self-aggrandizement, and most other human failings. I wasn't sure how far down that rabbit hole Saga was.

"Sorry. I forgot robots are people too." I tried to diffuse the situation.

"So, is she one step ahead of the cops?"

Saga answered, "Several steps. While you were jawing, I called up the front desk and got the clerk to describe the perp. I texted him the sketch for approval. Three tries and I have an excellent composite sketch of the assailant. Have a look at this."

The screen popped up a very detailed line drawing of a guy with a crew cut, wedge-shaped head, wide jawline, crooked nose and one cauliflower ear. The very stereotype of an over the hill boxer.

We hailed a cab, and while we were underway Saga reported that she had matched him to a photo on Facebook, but the name was obviously fake, and he had no friends.

"Email the sketch to the police. If he's local, there is a good chance they know him. By the way, how did you get the clerk to cooperate? I hope you didn't impersonate an officer."

"I promised the kid I would, like, blow him when he gets off work." Saga said this in a teenage, Valley-speak accent.

Billy laughed. "How are you going to deliver on that? Poor kid."

"I hired a pro to do it. You can get anything on the internet. I paid her from your Paypal account, Chan."

Billy laughed twice as hard. I choked.

The phone rang. It was Detective Penrose "We know the guy. Vladislav Kuchensky. Eastern European heavy, hangs around pool halls, runs numbers. I sent a squad to pick him up. I'm pretty sure you have the right guy, what we don't have is motivation. How did you get the sketch?"

"My assistant Saga drew it, based on the desk clerk's description of the perp. She promised him a blow job later."

Penrose laughed. "See, this is why P.I.s have an advantage. We aren't allowed to make promises like that. I'll let you know what we find out when we catch him. I'm impressed by your assistant's resourcefulness."

We went back to the marina. Billy was getting the boat ready for the delivery trip to San Francisco but planned to wait until we solved Gina's disappearance. I suspected it had something to do with one of the boats in the race. He gave Saga the URL of the Royal Victoria Yacht Club website where all the race details were listed. Then we ate some sandwiches, washed down with cold beer served by Afro's steward and chef, a middle-aged, totally bald guy called Curly Friesland.

Over lunch, Billy introduced the remaining crew. All the Corinthians and hangers-on who were just aboard for the race were gone, leaving only the paid professionals. Although I met them on race day, I had forgotten their names and positions. Besides Billy and Curly there were only four more.

Joe Riley, the mechanic/engineer, was a tall slim Kiwi, with a quiet demeanor, short black hair, and olive skin. I thought he was probably part Maori.

Vicky Ericson, the electrician, and only woman was a stocky redhead with a sassy attitude, and muscles that I found a bit intimidating, although I was a foot taller.

Gordon MacLeod was the navigator. He had longish gray hair and a hawk-like face with the clear blue eyes of a stereotypical airline pilot. I later found out that's exactly what he was until he retired.

King Chu was the sailing master and tactician. He

was Chinese but spoke with a Texan accent, which I found jarring. He was compact but muscular, in a Bruce Lee way. He seemed to be the strong, silent type.

I was introduced to all of them and we shook hands and made small talk. It was a minimal crew for a boat that size, but according to Billy, everyone but the steward could handle sails and steer.

After lunch, they went back to their jobs, and Billy and I sat down at the huge saloon table to make a timeline of events, and try to piece together what happened to Gina.

I started by asking Billy to draw a map of the marina, and show me which boats were located where. The bigger boats were on the northernmost float, and I figured Gina would have headed directly for Aphrodite, so it seemed likely she got taken on the way there. Naturally, I wanted to know which boats were on her route.

Saga searched the net and found some photos of the docks before the race, and that helped Billy a lot. You couldn't read the names on them, but he knew most of them on sight, based on shape, color, and rigging. I knew a few of them myself.

Saga's voice interrupted our mapping, "Billy, what does DNF mean? I'm looking at the Race results, the Royal Vic updates them in real time. Most of the boats have finished now."

"Did Not Finish. Usually, it means that a boat failed to cross the finish line before the time limit, but it could be a drop out for some other reason, like gear failure. The time limit isn't up yet."

"How about DNC? There are a couple of those."

"That means Did Not Compete. The boat failed to cross the start line for some reason. Sometimes a boat will enter the race and pay the registration fee, but then just not show up. The Swiftsure race is a long trip for some boats. We came from San Francisco. Most are closer, but many are from Portland or Seattle."

Saga said, "Was there a boat called Piratucu in the marina?"

Billy thought a moment, looked at his map then said, "No. I'm pretty sure it wasn't there. I know the boat, a Swan 65."

"The other DNC boat was Adonis."

"That was two boats behind us. It is a custom Wally 90. I'm surprised it's listed as DNC, I saw it leave the harbor just ahead of us on the morning of the race." A look of dismay came over Billy's ruddy countenance. "Do you think Gina was on board?"

"Quite possibly. The owner's name if Peter Tombolo. Do you know of any connection between him and Gina? I found his name mentioned in some old articles about her but they didn't explain the relationship."

Billy sighed. "I know the name, but I haven't met him. He was her first business partner, maybe more. I think the partnership ended badly, but that was long ago, before I was hired. You know, when Adonis was heading out, I noticed that there was only one person on deck. I assumed the rest of the crew was below decks getting their gear on for the race."

I jumped in, "Okay. He goes to the top of our

suspect list. See if you can find out where Adonis is right now. A boat that size would have an AIS transponder, and there are websites that show the location of AIS vessels." AIS stands for Automatic Identification System, and all commercial vessels and most larger yachts have it.

"On it," Saga snapped.

"You know, in Greek mythology, it was Aphrodite who chased Adonis, not the other way around," I mused.

# 10 TIGER'S VOYAGE

Balboa Yacht Club, twenty-three years ago…

The tiny Naples Sabot heeled to the Newport Harbor breeze, and Tiger shifted her weight to windward to keep it from capsizing. She was the smallest kid in the advanced class at the club. An advantage in light winds, but this time the wind was gusty and stronger than usual.

The two boats ahead of her were involved in a tacking duel on the way to the windward mark. Lisa and Mike were both tanned, blonde and blue-eyed, like male and female versions of the same person, even though they weren't related. SoCal bred them that way. They only cared about beating each other, nobody else existed. Tiger tacked away from them and called "Starboard" to indicate her right of way over the boy she was about to cut off.

"Tiggy, you're on port tack." The voice on the megaphone was the instructor in the Boston Whaler, idling near the mark. Of course, she knew she was on port tack, and didn't have the right of way. But the kid in the other boat was so conditioned to yield when someone called starboard, he fell away and let her pass in front of him. She grinned and pinched up as she approached the mark.

As Tiger pushed the tiller over with her right hand, she let the mainsheet slide through her left, smoothly pivoting around the big orange sphere that they used as a mark. As she bore away on the new course a big gust heeled the boat suddenly. She reacted fast and threw her weight to windward. The gust died abruptly and before she could throw herself back the gunwale went under. As the boat filled and capsized the aluminum boom flew across the cockpit and hit the side of her head.

The world was cold, blue and shimmering. Thoughts swam through her mind like a school of tropical fish, moving in unison then darting off in all directions.

The Omura refugee camp in Japan was the first home she remembered. Toddling around the camp, hiding behind the legs of the women, she was treated like a pet. An orphan, nobody knew how she got there. She had no name, but the Vietnamese women called her Con Cháu which just meant child. The women always gave her a hug or shared a morsel with her when she came by. She slept alone in her cot, guarded by an old woman with no family.

One day a husky boy of about nine was pushing and slapping a smaller boy. She launched herself at the bigger boy with such ferocity—nails scratching and tiny teeth biting—that he screamed and ran off. After that everyone called her Con Hổ. Tiger.

The boy she rescued became her first real friend. His name was Tommy Linh. They played together every day, and she became almost part of his family. He had a kindly mother and a grumpy older sister. Tiger ate with them and they moved her bed next to Tommy's. She and Tommy were inseparable, and ran, walked, and skipped around the camp hand in hand.

A year or so later Tommy's family was resettled in Yokohama. They wanted to take Tiger with them but the officials would not allow it. Tiger went back to sleeping by the old woman. For days, she cried herself to sleep. She never saw Tommy again.

When she was about five, a group of American women came to the camp. They were looking for children to adopt. Tiger was paler than most of the others and had dark brown hair. One woman, Edith Bergen, spent a long time with Tiger. She was much older than the other women and single. Tiger liked her, although she couldn't speak Vietnamese. By then Tiger spoke quite a bit of Japanese because of classes in the camp. A Japanese social worker acted as a translator, and they managed to communicate.

Tiger had no birth certificate, but the Japanese officials gave her an equivalent document listing her birthplace as Hanoi and birthday as June 1, 1979, based on a guess. Edith picked the name Gina Lee for the birth certificate.

Edith Bergen adopted her and they flew together to Los Angeles. Tiger understood she was being adopted and going to America. Almost all the Vietnamese in the camp had talked of going there, but she had no idea what it was like.

For the first two years, Edith spent every day teaching Tiger English, reading to her, and taking her for walks and drives to explore their Newport Beach neighborhood. She was a quick study and soon absorbed everything Edith felt competent to teach.

Then she was enrolled in Carden Hall, an elite private academy. They put her in grade 3 since she could already read and write at a high level, and she spoke fluent, unaccented English. There were a few other Asian kids in the school, and it didn't take her long to fit in. Within months, she was their leader.

Life in Newport Beach was affluent, comfortable

and safe, but Tiger never forgot the refugee camp. She challenged her teachers and read every book she could. She wanted to know everything about everything. She was the ideal student, one who truly wanted to learn. The only problem was, she kept skipping ahead, reading ahead, which made life hard for her teachers. They breathed a sigh of relief when she moved on to High School.

She was thirteen when Edith joined the Balboa Yacht Club because of their excellent Junior sailing program.

She felt strong hands pumping her chest, and warm lips on hers, forcing air into her lungs. She coughed and the lips withdrew. Her eyes fluttered open and she saw the instructor leaning over her.

"Tiggy! Thank God, you're alive. You'll be okay." The sound of his voice was reassuring. He touched the bump on the side of her head. His hand was warm and gentle. "We'd better get you to a hospital just in case. Maggie is calling your Mom."

He picked her up in his arms and carried her to the front seat of an old convertible, lowered her carefully into the seat and did up the seat belt. She touched his hand as he drove her to the hospital, "Thank you for saving my life, Chan."

He turned his head and smiled. "It's a life worth saving."

The next week when she went to the club for her sailing lesson, there was a new instructor. Nobody would tell her what happened to Chan. She didn't even know his full name.

Tiger ran behind the clubhouse and cried hot tears.

She vowed to herself to find him someday, but she was still just a kid. It would have to wait.

# 11 SEARCHING FOR DRAGONS

Billy and I continued work on the timeline. The race started on Saturday Morning. It was then Monday afternoon. Over 50 hours. If the Adonis headed straight out of Juan de Fuca at ten knots, her approximate cruising speed, she could be 500 miles from Victoria. If there was no crew except Tombolo on board she was probably motoring not sailing.

I picked up a compass and drew an arc on a chart of the area. It covered a range from Haida Gwaii in the North to the California border in the South. Billy commented, "That's a huge area. Even though this boat is much faster, there is no way we can catch up in any reasonable time. In fact, he could be in Mexico or Hawaii before we caught him. We need more exact information. Have you found anything yet Saga?"

"Some. The AIS is off, but the last recorded position was near the mouth of Juan de Fuca at about 3 PM Saturday. Adonis was on a northwest heading at 9.6 knots. Nothing after that."

Billy slapped himself on the forehead. "Damn, I forgot. All the boats in the race have a satellite transponder. The race committee sticks them to the deck. They don't have an on/off switch. The position of every boat in the race is shown on a real-time map on the internet."

In seconds, we had the map on the screen. There was a big cloud of dots in Victoria Harbour, and a few stragglers heading down Juan de Fuca. Only one boat was outside Juan de Fuca. Adonis.

"Billy, if you forgot the transponder maybe he did too. Show me what it looks like." He led me up on deck and pointed out the transponder, a small white dome, attached to the deck with double sided tape. It wasn't something you would normally notice, given the huge number of antennas, domes, and winches on those mega yachts. I unstuck the transponder and stuck it to the side of the dock we were tied to. That way if Adonis looked at the Royal Vic map, we would still show as tied up.

I called Detective Penrose and let her know what we had found. She listened carefully but didn't sound too helpful. "You don't have a shred of physical evidence to prove Ms. Lee is on that boat. According to the position you just gave me, Adonis is in International waters. She's registered in the Cayman Islands."

I could hear furious typing in the background, I guess she was Googling Adonis.

"Would the Coast Guard help?"

"I'll ask them to try and call Adonis on the radio. But they won't go chasing her based on this."

I digested that for a second then said, "Please don't have them call. I don't want to tip off Adonis."

She agreed. She also told me that they caught up with Vladislav Kuchensky, and he admitted drugging Tracy and taking her to the hotel. The story was that he was contacted by phone and agreed to do the job for eight hundred dollars. The money was in an envelope taped to the underside of a bench in a park near the Empress. He booked into the hotel in a phony name and paid cash. They were tracing the phone number but she doubted it would help.

After I hung up, I asked Billy to get Aphrodite ready for sea. Adonis was only a bit over a hundred miles away, and we decided to go after her. She was only moving at about 3 knots, heading Northwest up the coast of Vancouver Island.

"Billy, do you have any weapons on board?" I was considering our resources.

"No guns. We have fire axes, and several flare guns, including a high-power shotgun type. We have two dinghies in the garage, an RIB *(Rigid Inflatable Boat)* and a fiberglass Boston Whaler, both with 50 HP Hondas."

"Okay, that's something anyway. While you get the boat ready I'll collect my clothes from the Empress and see if I can buy any other useful gear."

Saga spoke up. "I have a list of things to buy at the Stealth Shop on Government Street."

"What sort of things?"

"I'll show you when we get there."

We headed out. I checked out of the Empress and then we grabbed a cab to the Stealth Shop, a place I had never heard of before. They had an amazing array of spy cameras, listening devices, and drones.

It was the drones that interested Saga, she spoke from my pocket. "Show me your longest-range drone."

The clerk looked startled but then he squinted at my sunglasses. His face relaxed as he recognized them, the first person to do so. "Boss on Skype, eh?"

I nodded. He pointed over in the corner. The five-rotor drone was a least six feet across. I nixed it.

"Nothing I can't carry in a duffel bag. I have to take it onboard a small boat."

Saga said, "How about the smallest drone with an HD camera?"

The clerk, who according to his name tag, was called Brad, showed us a small quad-rotor drone with an excellent camera.

"You don't need the controller if you use the phone app over Wi-Fi. However, it is much easier to fly with the controller. It is included anyway."

"Can I try it? Switch it on. Okay, I see its Wi-Fi server. Connected. I found the manual online. Okay taking off." Saga was running through a checklist.

The drone rose straight up, swiveled, and the phone screen showed a fairly crisp video of me standing there stupidly. It then flew around the shop, hid behind shelves, and landed back where it started.

"Wow, your boss sure learns fast. She must have flown one before." I had no comment.

"We'll take two. I want something ground based as well." Saga was all business.

We walked out with the two drones and a tiny tank with a camera and a "gun" which fired a red laser beam like the laser pointer teachers use. It moved almost silently and could pick up sound as well as video.

We moved on to an electronics store where we bought two powerful battery-operated Bluetooth speakers. Saga picked them, and played the 1812 Overture through them, the bit with the cannons. They sounded amazing, as well they might since they cost more than the drones.

Then we got a cab back to the marina. Joe came out to help me with all the stuff. As soon as we were on board, the lines were cast off and we were away.

"We went out to the fuel dock and filled the tanks while you were gone. We usually race with nearly empty tanks to save weight. We have a range of about 3000 miles under power and enough food and water for at least a month." Billy noted as we motored past the cruise ship dock and out into Juan de Fuca Strait.

"What have we got for power?" I'm a boat guy, and I like to know these things.

"Twin 1500 HP Deutz diesels, with feathering propellers. She'll do sixteen knots flat out." He pushed the throttles forward and the big yacht surged ahead. Soon we were cruising at fourteen knots. I calculated it would take us ten hours or so to get near to Adonis, assuming they stayed at the same speed.

"Uh-oh. I just thought of a major problem. Saga depends completely on an internet connection to the server. It can be Wi-Fi or cell data, but it is essential to her operation. We'll be out of cell range"

Billy chuckled, "You are on the right boat. This year we spent over a quarter mil on a new communications setup. We have worldwide high-speed satellite internet, and our own cell phone system. Until this year we used walkie-talkies on board but now we use cell phones, which we all carry anyway. Saga, just connect to network Afro-1."

"Connected. What is the range?"

"In open water, at least 10 miles, less in harbor, but then you can use the phone company. Your phone number stays the same and incoming calls will reach you."

"Thanks, Billy, that could be a life saver. I'm glad to know Saga will keep working."

"Don't thank me, thank Gina. She owns the company that installed the system, and this is the only private yacht in the world that has it. The other systems are being installed on cruise ships."

Curly served up an excellent dinner featuring a rack of lamb. No alcohol was served in deference to our mission. It felt good to be on the chase, even though we were not absolutely sure we were after the right guy. Over dinner, I ask Billy something that had been bothering me.

"Why do you think he is going so slow?"

"Most likely because nobody is keeping watch. If there is no lookout, you heave to or go slow to avoid hitting anything. There are big logs floating around in addition to other ships. When it gets dark my guess is he'll be running without lights. He'll still show on radar, but without AIS ships won't be able to identify him. They might call on VHF but he probably won't answer. At the speed Adonis is traveling right now, a log wouldn't do any damage."

I wasn't sure what to make of that. It could mean Tombolo had no other crew, or it could mean they were goons, not sailors.

"Does that mean we can sneak up on him?"

"He is almost certain to have set a radar alarm, to tell him if another ship gets too close. We normally keep ours at 5 miles, if you make it more sensitive than that it tends to give false alarms." Billy had a good understanding of the issue.

"Is there anything we can do to make us harder to see?"

"Yes, big as Afro is, the fiberglass hull and carbon mast don't show well on radar. I can have the crew take down the radar reflector after we are out of the Strait. There is too much traffic around here. And we can set the AIS to transmit the name of another ship. We can't change the MMSI number but that wouldn't mean anything to him."

"Great, let's do that. If we call the ship M.S. Sea Gray, I'm pretty sure Gina would know it's us if she should happen to see the chart plotter."

Saga spoke up again. "The transponder just went off. He must have found it and thrown it overboard. Don't worry, I found another way to track Adonis, in fact, two ways. Firstly, I hacked into a spy satellite which passes over every couple of hours and identified the boat in the photos. It will be dark when we catch up, but they have a satellite internet dome just like Afro's. Tombolo probably doesn't know it reports the latitude and longitude to the network every ten minutes. I hacked into that too. The course hasn't changed. I don't think he knows we are following him."

"Great work Saga. Call the helmsman and tell him the new coordinates so he can mark them on the chart plotter. Then see if you can get me the plans of Adonis, I want to learn the layout."

A few minutes later we had the plans on the big screen TV in the saloon. Saga found an article about the boat in Superyacht Magazine which had photos too. The interior was very spare, all straight lines and hard edges, which is typical of the Wally style. Unlike most of their designs, Adonis had a shelter over the forward end of the cockpit, making it more suitable for ocean sailing. Despite their large size, most Wallys were used for day-sailing in the Med.

I was trying to decide where the most likely place to keep a prisoner would be. The engine room was centrally located beneath the cockpit, and a rope locker was directly ahead of it. On the starboard side of the engine room there was a large galley, more or less a restaurant kitchen. On the port side, there were two crew staterooms with upper and lower bunks and a shared head between them.

Ahead of the companionway ladder, there was an enormous full-width saloon area with long settees, armchairs, and coffee tables which folded out to become dining tables. The owner's stateroom was just forward of the saloon, on the port side. It had a king-size bed on one side, and a twin bed opposite, with only a narrow space between them. There was a large ensuite head with separate shower and Jacuzzi tub.

I considered the possibility that he would confine her there, but I was inclined to think that was his personal space. I went back to examining the plans. Just then Joe came in.

"I have been meaning to tell you. I worked on Adonis for a delivery trip from the Med to Aruba, long before I worked on Afro. I know the layout pretty well."

"Can you think of a likely place where a prisoner would be kept?"

"Oh yeah. You see the theater room opposite the owner's stateroom? We watched Blu-Ray movies in there a few times, Big projection screen, and a great sound system. The crew always referred to it as The Dungeon. One day when I was off watch I snooped around it because I wondered where the name came from. I found out the screen folds up to the ceiling and behind it is a wall with restraints. There were whips and other stuff I didn't recognize behind sliding panels on either side of the room. With the screen up and those panels open it did look like a dungeon, but clean and modern, not medieval. I'm almost certain that's where you'll find her." Joe sounded confident.

"Thanks, Joe, great information. I think you're right. What kind of guy is Tombolo?"

"I never met him. But the crew seemed afraid of him, they did everything by the book, even though he wasn't on board."

"Saga, I'm going to try to get some sleep. You practice flying the drones, then get one of the crew to plug everything in to charge."

"Yassuh Boss. I be doin' it." A pretty good Stepin Fetchit imitation.

"And quit busting my balls!"

I went to the guest stateroom that Curly had assigned me, showered and slipped into the soft bed under a down duvet. I couldn't help feeling guilty that I was so comfortable while Gina was probably anything but. If only I hadn't slept in that morning, Gina and I would have walked down the dock together and she would have been safe. Or, more likely, if invited aboard Adonis, I would have gone with her, and now I'd be captive too.

Black thoughts swirled in my head as I drifted off.

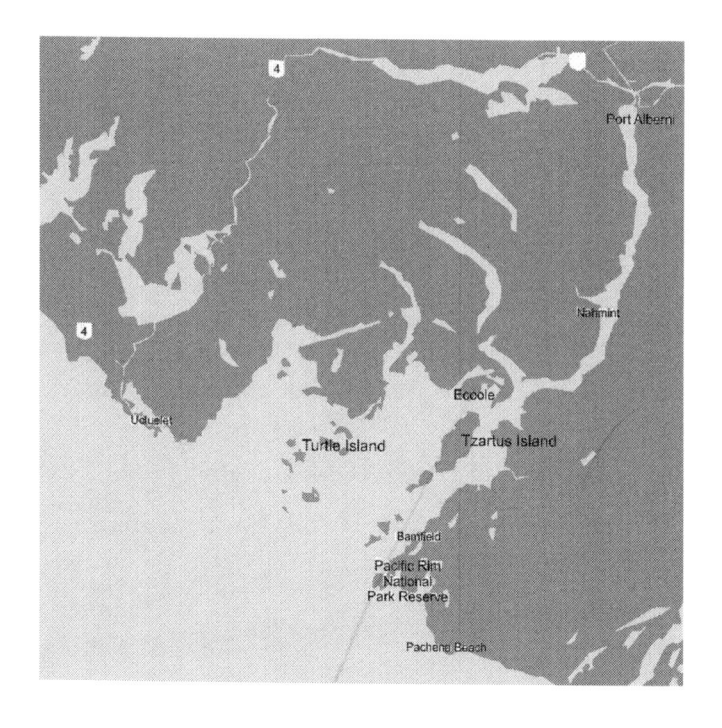

Map of Barkley Sound

# 12 BY THE SWORD

*I was cold and naked, tied by chains to a rough stone wall. An angry faced Japanese guy in a gray uniform shouted at me, then threw a bucket of filthy water in my face. He unchained me and dragged me over to a wooden block and forced my head down onto it. A tall woman in a samurai costume stood before me. She raised a gleaming sword, then stopped beside me, all I could see were her sandaled feet. She shouted something and I heard the swish of the blade through the air.*

I woke up with a jerk, my body drenched in sweat. It took a few moments for me to remember where I was. The boat had developed a long slow rolling motion and a quick pitch. We were out in the open North Pacific. I waited for my thumping heart to slow down, then looked out the port near my bunk. The sky was clear but black, and I could see millions of stars between big rollers which swept by majestically, topped with the occasional white crest.

Time for action. I quickly dressed in warm clothes and headed up to the saloon. There was nobody there except Vicky, who was seated at the instrument console, looking at the radar screen,

"Hi Vicky. How far are we from Adonis now?"

"Just over 7 miles. She hasn't changed course at all, must be on autopilot."

It was about 3 AM. I called Billy on his cell phone.

"Taylor. What's up?"

"Billy, it's Chan. We are close enough now. I'll need two crew members, Joe—since he knows Adonis—and whoever your best dinghy handler is."

"That would be Vicky, but she has been on watch for the last three hours. I'll get King, he is good too, and tough as nails. I'll be up in a couple of minutes with the crew." Billy sounded ready to go.

"Saga, can you email a brief description of our activities so far to the gang? Just in case something untoward happens, I'd like them to be up to date."

"Oui, Mon Capitan."

When the crew arrived in the saloon I briefed them on my plan.

"Three of us will take the RIB and come up fast

behind Adonis. A dinghy won't show on radar in the ocean swells, it will be lost in the wave clutter. We'll board by the stern platform. Joe and I will take Saga onboard, along with the drones, LED flashlights, and flare pistols. King will wait by the dinghy in case we have to make a quick getaway."

"Evidence points to Tombolo being alone, as Adonis has held constant speed and course since we spotted it. I think he's below decks with Gina, not keeping watch. But we can't count on that. Also, we have no idea what arms he might have. Do you know, Joe?"

"There was a locked weapon compartment on board, but I never saw inside," Joe said.

"Okay, we better assume he has a gun, and there could be booby traps. I want Saga to fly her drones around the ship before we go in, to see if she can spot any threats. Saga, can you add to the plan?"

"Yes. You better put my phone and the drones in a waterproof bag in case we get wet on the way over. And bring the Bluetooth speakers, I can use them to make distracting noises. It would be good if we could turn off the lights on board if we have to storm him."

"I know where the circuit breakers are, so I can cut the power if needed," Joe added.

"Okay, sounds like we are ready. Let's get our gear on."

We dressed in lightweight waterproofs, black watch caps, and sea boots. Luckily there was a good selection of foul weather gear on board, including boots that fitted my size twelve feet. The jackets had bright yellow reflective stripes, as did the inflatable life vests we put on. Not exactly stealthy, but that was what we had.

Billy slowed Afro down to a couple of knots so we could launch the dinghy. There was about a twelve knot Northwest wind, and the water was fairly smooth aft of the big yacht, but there was a substantial swell rolling in, so we had to be careful.

King pressed the button that opened the dinghy garage in a whir of hydraulics. He hadn't said a single word yet, just nods and grunts.

He grabbed a portable controller from just inside the garage and held another button, which caused the RIB to slide out. It was pretty substantial, about 15 feet long, with a center console, folding radar arch, and seating for about 8 people. Fuel tanks for the outboard were built in. King jumped in and started the quiet Honda. I got in and Joe cast off the bow line as he came aboard. King put the engine in reverse and backed off slowly.

Joe erected the radar arch and locked it in place. King switched on the radar, and we identified the blip that had to be Adonis, about 5 miles away. He opened the throttle part way and the boat jumped up on plane quickly. I figured it was capable of 30 knots, but given the swells, we were running at about half that. Even so, we were getting wet when we hit a bigger than average wave. It was hard to steer around them in the dark. King slowed down a bit, which helped.

In about twenty minutes we saw a white light where Adonis should be, and as we got closer we could see that her running lights were on. That was a surprise. A yacht shows three running lights at night when sailing. Forward, red to port, green to starboard.

Aft, a single white light. When motoring an additional white light on the front of the mast is shown. The light we saw was her stern light.

"Saga, please text Billy and let him know we are close, and that her running lights are on."

"Done." No sarcasm.

There was no sign of life on deck. The dinghy garage was closed, but a large swim platform and steps led to deck level. Boarding would be easy as the soft tubes of the RIB would take the impact, and the waves and wind would muffle the sound of our motor.

King slowed the motor and crept up close to the transom, then opened the throttle a little to push the bow against Adonis. Joe jumped out and threw the bow line around a stern cleat, but didn't tie it off. Instead, he led it back to the dinghy so it could be let fly from there. He knew what he was doing. I felt a growing sense of trust and confidence in the two of them.

The Royal Vic's transponder was still glued to the after deck. I guessed that it had stopped because of a dead battery rather than being tossed overboard.

I slipped aboard. Adonis was a pretty steady platform. I opened the waterproof bag and got out the drones. With my Bluetooth earpiece, I could hear Saga and whisper to her without alerting the enemy, as I was now thinking of Tombolo.

The cockpit was large and open, with just a small shelter at the forward end. We huddled under it. The companionway doors were open, so Saga flew one drone inside. We could see the images on her screen.

The boat was lit by dim LED footlights along the walkways, but all the overhead lights were off. Still, the drone had good night vision.

The main saloon was clear. Saga flew the drone into the galley and the crew's quarters, but there was no sign of life. The only sound we could hear was the rumble of the big diesel, which was turning over slowly, just above idle.

Next, she went forward. The door to the master stateroom was open, and she flew in there. Nothing. When she flew out we could see light coming under the doorway opposite. The Dungeon. I suggested she check the rest of the staterooms forward before we took any action. Again, no sign of life.

"Chan, on your way in, put the one speaker at the forward end of the saloon, and the other right outside the door of the theater. Tell Joe to cut the power at exactly 3:55, then head to the theater. You should already be there when the lights go off. I'll create a diversion. If the door is unlocked, throw it open and step to the side in case he shoots." Saga was now the one giving the orders.

We did as she said.

A few seconds before 3:55 a booming voice shouted. "Police! Freeze! Put your hands on your head."

It was the cop who arrested me in Victoria, so realistic I almost put my hands on my head. Then the lights went out. I flung the door open and stepped aside, but no shots rang out. I shone my light into the room and Saga flew the drone in. Nothing.

"Joe, there is nobody here. Put the lights back on

and let's see what we have."

When the lights came on I saw what did indeed look like a dungeon. The movie screen was folded up, and the wall behind it had an array of hooks, leg restraints, and straps. But what chilled my blood was a felt marker outline of a woman on the wall. Hands above the head, where there was a hook, then below the outline of the head, a neck strap. Then a waist strap, and two ankle clamps. The shape gave me no doubt that Gina had been confined here. But where was she now?

There was an envelope taped to the neck restraint. Inside was a USB stick. I put it in my pocket.

"What do we do now?"

"Good question Joe. I wonder what kind of person abandons a ten-million-dollar yacht as a decoy. Any ideas Saga?"

"Game theory would suggest that the objective is of such high value that the yacht is a minor strategic sacrifice."

"Okay. Call Billy and tell him we are going to take command of Adonis and take her to an anchorage in Barkley Sound. We'll lock her up and leave her there for now. Joe, do you know how to open the dinghy garage?"

"Sure."

"Okay, open it and see if it is empty. I'm guessing it is. If possible, put the RIB in there and bring King onboard."

I searched the boat thoroughly. Plenty of food and water, nearly full fuel tanks. Everything neat and tidy.

The only clue to what happened is the USB stick. I didn't find a computer onboard. Laptops are what you find these days, even on Superyachts, so I suppose they were removed when the crew left. Joe and King came back in.

"We put the RIB in the garage. Plenty of room, their dinghy is gone," Joe said. King just nodded agreement.

"Joe, you're the Captain of Adonis for now, since you know how to run her. Let's set a course for Turtle Island, there's a safe anchorage for a boat this size. King, you are the first mate."

Within a few minutes we were underway for Barkley Sound, and I sat down. Adrenaline had kept me moving, but now I gave in to despair. I put my head in my hands and let the tears flow. I had no idea where Gina could be. I just hoped she was alive.

## 13 TURTLE IN PARADISE

*"You can swim all day in the Sea of Knowledge and still come out completely dry. Most people do."* -- Norton Juster

By the time we were in Barkley Sound, I was feeling a bit better. I had put Saga to work compiling a complete dossier on Tombolo, his business connections and any dirt she could find on him.

When I went on deck, it was dawn, and a thin mist was rising off calm water. Aphrodite was right behind us and I could see Billy at the wheel. Soon we were at Turtle Island and the anchor chain was rattling out over the drum. Joe set the anchor in reverse, then shut down the engine.

Under maritime law, we had a right to claim salvage of the Adonis, and given that she was abandoned, we might well end up owning her. But that seemed really trivial to me.

We locked up the yacht and King slid our RIB out of the garage. It was a subdued crew that went back aboard Aphrodite.

I called Detective Penrose and told her where to find Adonis. I described our rescue mission, leaving out Saga's part.

"Chan, you're having all the fun, while I'm stuck here. Too bad you didn't find Gina, but it sounds as if she is alive. Anyway, we'll send a forensics team to Adonis before we have her towed in for impound. The courts will decide what happens after that. Let me know what you find on the USB stick."

Billy directed me to his office, where a laptop was attached to a big LCD monitor. I plugged in the USB stick. There was just one photo on it. It showed Gina, apparently unconscious, still wearing her sailing clothes. She was tied to the wall in the same position as the outline we found. There were no visible wounds, which gave me hope. There was also a text file. I opened it.

If you want to see Gina again, get two billion US ready to be wire transferred. Email when the money is available.

The email address was a random sequence of numbers, at one of the free email providers anyone can get. I called Billy over and showed him the photo and the note.

"Look at the ransom demand. Is there any way to pay that?"

"I doubt it. Gina is wealthy—I'm guessing in the hundreds of millions—but two billion? Not likely. We can contact her accountant and her lawyers and see what they say." Billy was looking stressed. I'm sure I was too.

I emailed the photo and the note to Detective Penrose. It didn't give us a clue as to Gina's present whereabouts. I was hoping that Saga could come up with something. First I conferred with Billy about our next move. We decided to go back to port in Victoria.

Next, I had Saga go back over the AIS and satellite tracks for Adonis, to try and establish the time and position where she was abandoned. That would be when she slowed down and started the course we found her on. I wanted to know what ships were within dinghy range.

It was also possible that they had gone ashore at Sooke or some other point on the coast. I discounted this possibility since having taken the trouble to head into International waters, why go back to Canadian soil? It didn't make sense.

"Okay, Chan. There was only one ship within 5 miles of the Adonis at the time of abandonment. Persephone, 77,000 tons, registered in Panama but bound for Tokyo. Currently about 310 miles offshore, traveling at 12.7 knots. At that rate, she will arrive in about eleven days."

"Saga, keep track of that ship. Try and find out who owns it, what it is carrying and get the plans if you can. What did you find on Tombolo?"

"I found a lot of information, too much to read out. I'll print it for you."

Moments later I could hear the laser printer in Billy's office start up. "Just the highlights for now."

"Born in San Francisco in 1975, American father, Japanese mother. A very rare family name, I didn't find anybody else with that name in North America. He apparently inherited a fortune, invested in real estate and technology companies, Estimated net worth of $140 million. Speaks Japanese as well as English, and travels there frequently."

"Okay, better do the same sort of search on Gina Lee, and print those results too."

I didn't have much to do until we got to Victoria, so I checked my phone and text messages. My mother left a message saying Brophy had fixed her computer for her. My ex-wife called to ask if I had her photo albums, Charlie called to invite me to dinner.

Feinman wanted to meet for coffee, and Ollie called to ask what I thought about Maseratis. All of them wanted to know if we had found Gina. I called them all back, except for my ex-wife.

Having brought my friends up to date, I had a shower and lay down to nap. I tried to imagine why Gina was kidnapped in such an elaborate way. She didn't have a bodyguard. Why involve a ten-million-dollar yacht, then abandon it. The ransom demand was a bluff, clearly, there was no way they could collect such a sum.

I was left with several theories, which I tried out on Saga.

"Saga, my first theory is that Gina's kidnap was a revenge thing, and the ransom wasn't important, it was just a distraction. If they wanted her dead, whoever they were, it could easily have been done in Victoria, or on the yacht."

Saga replied, "If that is so, we should be able to find a motive when we compare Tombolo's profile with Gina's. I'm still collecting data for that."

"What if Gina has something else they want, and the ransom is a delaying tactic? They could be torturing it out of her right now."

"Again, a complete inventory of Gina's assets should turn up something."

"Maybe I'm the target, and Gina is the bait?"

Saga snorted. I had no idea software could snort. "You really think you are that important? That doesn't add up since you would have been easy to snatch at almost any time."

"Okay, what do you think the target is?"

"Elementary, my dear Watson. It's me they are after. Clearly, Moriarty is behind this."

I didn't have an answer for that, so I put my head down and dozed off. Saga woke me as we approached Victoria. I went up on deck to talk with Billy.

"Billy, I'm going to fly back to Vancouver and get a plan together to rescue Gina. First, I'll need to talk with her accountant and her lawyers. I'll need complete honesty. Do you trust me enough to try and set that up?"

"Well Chan, after what you did last night, I believe you want to help Gina, just as much as I do. I already spoke to the lawyer and the accountant and they are expecting to hear from you. They'll expect you to use the word *weather* in your first sentence."

He gave me the phone numbers. I decide to wait until I got home before calling. I went to my cabin and packed up my things, including Saga, the drones, and speakers. Then I shook hands with the crew and headed up the dock. While I was waiting for a cab, Detective Penrose called.

"Chan, forensics found some blood in the dungeon, just a few drops, but we are sending it for a DNA test. I'm sending a man down to her boat to get a sample of Gina's hair for comparison. Will that be a problem?"

"Talk to Billy, I'm sure he'll help you. There is bound to be some in her cabin on board. I'm going back to Vancouver to try and determine the next step. We think she is being held aboard a ship heading to Japan."

"Is she Japanese? I can never tell by just looking, and I have only seen her in photos."

"She told me she was a Vietnamese orphan, but that hasn't been verified yet. Lee isn't a Japanese name. Not Vietnamese either, but there were a lot of ethnic Chinese in Vietnam, and many of them became boat people."

"By the way, Peter Tombolo has a record in California, so we have his prints and a DNA profile," Cary said.

"Really? What did he do?"

"Simple assault. He slapped a clerk in a Lululemon store. Apparently, she said something he objected to. No jail time, just a fine."

"Just a moment Carly," I spoke to the cab which had just arrived. "Heli-jet please.

It is a far cry from that to kidnapping."

"It is possible that he isn't your perp. We haven't been able to find anybody who can positively identify him as the man seen onboard Adonis. She was dark the night before the Swiftsure when all the other boats were lit up and partying. Nobody thought anything of it, they just thought the crew was partying on another boat or at the Yacht Club. I called his office in California, and his secretary told me he was at the race, and they haven't heard from him since. They have reported him missing."

After I hung up I started reading through the printouts on Tombolo. He sounded like a rich playboy type, but he did have a company called Adonis Industries, which was also the owner of the yacht. It was privately held, and he was the only director. No official figures but Forbes magazine put his personal net worth at $260 million. I didn't think he needed to collect ransom to pay his phone bill.

Saga said, "I have an update. The MS Persephone is a Roll-On-Roll-Off car carrier, launched in 2011. She delivered a cargo of 2912 new Toyota cars of various models to New Westminster BC. She is heading back to Tokyo mostly empty. Crew of 15, all Japanese, despite the Greek name."

I had a sudden thought. "Persephone was Aphrodite's rival for Adonis. She was Queen of the Underworld, bride of Hades, King of the underworld. She was an innocent girl named Kora, daughter of Demeter, the harvest goddess. She was kidnapped and raped by the lonely Hades. Zeus forced Hades to let her go back to her mother. He fed her a pomegranate seed, and she was transformed into the goddess Persephone, as powerful as Hades himself."

Saga said, "Yes, I read about it. Greek mythology. There are several versions of the myth. In one version Adonis spends half the year with Aphrodite and the other half with Persephone,"

"Actually, Aphrodite was in love with him, but he was killed by a wild boar, and descended to the Underworld. Aphrodite convinced Zeus to send him back to her six months of the year." I may have read a few books of Greek mythology in my youth. "The names of the three ships seem an unlikely coincidence. We need to find out who owns Persephone."

"It is a numbered corporation registered in the Cayman Islands, and it is the only ship they own. It is on charter to the Toyota Motor Company, but the crew is provided by the owners."

"Saga, can you try to find out the name of the Captain, and his background. It seems definite there is a Japanese connection. Persephone is bound for Tokyo and Tombolo was half Japanese. What have you got on Gina?"

"For somebody so wealthy, she doesn't have much of a public profile. The only biography I found was an article in the San Francisco Chronicle, part of a series on powerful women. It was pretty much what she told you. Forbes magazine estimates her net worth at 1.2 Billion., I found a few photos of her with Peter Tombolo a while back, but no mention of a business connection."

"Okay, print whatever you have, including the photos."

Saga added, "By the way, Gina's disappearance has hit the news. They are reporting that she was seen dining with an unknown man at the Empress on the night before she disappeared. I guess that was you. Her personal assistant Tracy Wagner confirmed that Gina was missing, but offered no further information. There are lots of theories on the internet, all of them nonsense."

When we got to Vancouver, Ollie picked us up at the chopper in his latest car, a brand-new Rosso Alfa Romeo 4C. It was an amazing looking vehicle, short but wide, low and very, very red. The tiny trunk barely held my laptop computer. I folded myself into the passenger seat with luggage on my lap.

"Chan, I got the payout from ICBC, and I couldn't resist this. It is just so beautiful." Unlike the French stereotype, Ollie gives his greatest passion to cars and boats.

"Hi Ollie, great to see you too. Gina sends her regards from her cage on the Persephone." I was a little grumpy.

"Huh? Oh, right. I guess you want to go to your office."

"Yes, and step on it."

I shouldn't have said that. The G-forces we underwent getting to my office would put the Space Shuttle to shame. Ollie tapped the paddle shifters like Louis Hamilton. The crackling exhaust of the Alfa blatted sonorously on every upshift. If it wasn't for the headrest I'd have needed a neck brace after that ride.

I waited until we were safely upstairs before I filled him in on the tale of three ships, and the Greek myths associated with Aphrodite, Adonis, and Persephone.

"I don't understand why all this is happening. You won the Swiftsure, Gina was kidnapped, her personal assistant was tied up. Adonis was abandoned and you developed an interest in Greek gods?"

"Yes, yes, and yes. And don't forget, there seems to be a Japanese connection too."

"Wow, I hate to tell you, but this is sounding more like James Bond than the life of a geeky software developer. And wasn't the Persephone Nick's log salvage boat on the Beachcombers?"

"More yesses. But not only do I not have a license to kill, I wouldn't know how to do it anyway. And I don't speak Japanese."

Just then the phone rang. It was Carly Penrose. "I

have some surprising information for you. The DNA tests came back. The blood from the Adonis wasn't Gina's. It belonged to Peter Tombolo. But, as they say in the infomercials, there's more. Gina isn't Vietnamese, she's 50% Japanese, 25% Northern European, 25% Chinese. Tombolo is 50% Japanese. The same 50%."

"Okay, that's a surprise. So, both of them had Japanese mothers?"

"No. They both had the same Japanese mother. They are half-siblings."

I had to sit down.

# 14 ALMOST A FAMILY

I was stunned. Did Gina Lee and Peter Tombolo know they had the same mother? Was there an incestuous relationship? Maybe Tombolo was kidnapped too?

Ollie had to go back to his office. Kimi was texting him about a problem with the CNC machine. Ollie was always working to a deadline, but he worked best under pressure. No deadline, no work. He would be out sailing Disturbance or driving his exotic car too fast somewhere.

Feinman was almost always busy with multiple projects, which he worked on in the short spaces between coffee dates, music festivals, and dance sessions. Charlie was the most likely to have time to talk, so I called him.

He answered right away, "Charlie Quant."

"Chandler Gray. Charlie, I'm thinking we may need to indulge in some high seas piracy."

I filled him in on the situation with the Persephone. He thought for a bit and answered slowly.

"Why a rescue at sea? Why not fly to Tokyo and intercept the ship when she docks. You could report the kidnapping to the Japanese police."

"I did think of that, but the kind of people who can orchestrate something as complex and expensive as this probably have power over the police. I'm not willing to take that chance. The North Pacific is not exactly a pirate zone, so they won't be expecting an attack."

"They have a pretty big head start. How can we catch up with them?"

"Gina has a private jet. Years ago, flying to Japan from here I noticed we flew over the Aleutian Islands. The shipping route has got to pass close to them. Dutch Harbor on Unalaska Island has an airport. I want you to find out if there is a boat in Dutch Harbor we can charter. It doesn't have to be very big, but a speed of twenty knots or more would be good."

"Any other requirements?"

"A fiberglass hull would be good but we may have to settle for aluminum. And she'll need a good dinghy. I'll call you again after I look at the photos of Persephone."

After I hung up, I asked Saga to print out any pictures and drawings of Persephone she could find.

"The printer is out of magenta ink. Could you change it for me?"

Luckily there was some printer ink in the drawer of the printer table. Unluckily it was for a different printer…

"Saga, just put the pictures up on the screen of my PC. The ScreenShare app can do that."

"Okay Boss."

While I was waiting, I scratched my head. My right hand came away bloody. I touched my scalp but couldn't find a wound. I felt a sense of panic as I went to the bathroom to wash my hands. It didn't wash off. That's when I remembered removing the Magenta ink cartridge from the printer. I wondered how I would deal with real blood…

When I came out of the bathroom the pictures were on screen. The Persephone was massive, high and boxy. Since it was a RO-RO, there were no cranes on deck, and it had a helicopter pad.

"Saga, check for me if there have been any successful pirate raids against a ship of that type."

"Negative. There was one attempt off the Somali coast in 2012 but the pirates couldn't get aboard, and they gave up. Those ships are too high to just throw a heaving line to."

"Okay, get Billy on Skype and I'll see what we can come up with. I think he and his crew can help. Wait, before that, we better get Gina's lawyer on the line. His name is…"

"Jonathan Roberts. I have his number. Calling now."

"Roberts, McLaren, and Philips. How may I direct your call?"

I picked up the phone. "This is Chandler Gray. I need to speak to Jonathan Roberts urgently, it concerns Gina Lee and the weather."

Roberts came on the line. I could picture him in a gray pinstripe suit, seated behind a polished mahogany desk high in a San Francisco skyscraper. I brought him up to date, although he seemed quite well informed already. His cultured voice displayed just a hint of concern for Gina's safety.

"Miss Lee left us an envelope with instructions in case of her disappearance or kidnapping. In essence, it says not to pay ransom, but authorizes almost unlimited expenditure on rescue and liberation."

I was glad to hear that. I filled him in on my plans, and he agreed to okay whatever expenditures we needed, as long as we had proper documentation. He also agreed to transfer $100,000 to my bank account, based on what Billy and Tracy had told him about me. This was to cover any expenditures requiring cash.

Saga got Billy on Skype, and the rest of the crew was with him.

"Hi Billy. Thanks for talking with Roberts. We're making a plan to rescue Gina. First, are you and your crew willing and available to help?"

Billy said, "We'll do whatever is needed. Gina is loved and respected by the crew."

A chorus of Oh Yeah and Right On from the background reinforced his statement. But I had more.

"Do any of you have a military background?"

"I was a US Navy Seal." I recognized King Chu's Texas drawl.

"I was a sergeant in the New Zealand's Special Operations Forces," Joe said, "It is patterned on the British SAS."

Billy added, "Vicky is an amazing boat handler. And David can pilot anything that flies. I can skipper anything that floats."

"Fantastic! Here is my plan, open to your suggestions and improvements. I think we can intercept the Persephone near the Aleutians. I have my buddy Charlie arranging to charter the most suitable boat we can find in Dutch Harbor. We'll use Gina's jet to get us there. Her lawyer has given the go ahead. I'm hoping we can get some weapons. We would get within a couple of miles of the ship, then take a Zodiac over for boarding. I'm hoping Joe and King will have some idea how to do that."

"We had a thing called a Bridger Line Throwing gun in the navy. The trouble is, it just throws a line. We need something that throws a grappling hook we can then send over a rope ladder with. The deck of that ship is about fifty feet off the water." This is by far the longest speech I have ever heard from King.

Joe said, "Resqmax makes a pneumatic line thrower that can throw a grappling hook with a line attached 80 feet straight up. That would be my choice."

"Thanks, Joe, that sounds like the right kit. Saga, can you order two of those with at least two ladders and grappling hook sets? Get them air expressed to Dutch Harbor, I'm sure you can find someone there to accept them."

"Hai Taishou." Saga in a deep Samurai voice.

"I have another question for all of you. I don't want to kill or maim the crew of the ship. Is there a gas that we could deploy through the vents that would knock them out temporarily?"

Laughter all round. Billy answered that one. "The short answer is NO. There are lots of substances that can do this in controlled individual applications, like chloroform. But only in the movies is there a gas that can knock everybody out without harm. Chances are either they won't get enough to put them out, or they'll get too much and die. Killing everybody is easy, not hurting them is harder."

"I was afraid of that. Any suggestions?"

Joe said, "The best bet is stealth. If we come up from astern in a zodiac, they probably won't see us. A ship at sea is looking ahead, not behind, and the radar beams will be well above us. After midnight, there will likely be only three or four crew on the bridge. The rest will be in their cabins, sleeping or watching TV. If we take the bridge first, we could just tie up the rest of the crew in the cabins. They won't be expecting piracy in the North Pacific, so they probably won't be armed."

"How many people do we need to do the job? "

"I think we have enough with our crew plus you. We'll need gags and zip ties for the crew."

'Thanks Joe. I'll get Saga to send you the plans of the Persephone so we know where they are likely to be holding Gina. Any more info on the Persephone, Saga?"

"There are 18 crew registered, four officers, two engineers, one cook, and the rest able-bodied seaman. The Captain is Hideaki Tanaka. I have the names of the crew; they are all Japanese. I will email them to you and Billy. Tanaka was in the Japanese Maritime Self Defense force for twenty years and retired two years ago at the age of forty-two. Captaining the Persephone is his retirement job. The rest of the crew all have a merchant marine background, nothing military.

"The ship's manifest shows it going back to Japan nearly empty. There are seven antique cars, two-wheeled containers of car parts, and one large motorhome made by Entegra."

Billy said, "I know those. They are built on a bus chassis, and cost the best part of a million dollars."

"Saga, check the specs on that. It could be where Gina is being held. It would have large tanks, and is probably self-sufficient for quite a while, just like a boat." I knew that would take only a few seconds.

"According to the website it has 150-gallon diesel fuel, 100-gallon water, 60-gallon gray water and 40-gallon black water tanks. It has a generator and large battery capacity. It has both a fridge and a freezer. By my calculation two people could live for at least ten days on board, assuming sufficient food. "

Billy said, "I'm pretty sure that's where Gina would be kept. The crew may not even know she's there. They have very little reason to go down to the truck deck when they are under way."

This gave me a thought. "Is there a way we could get into the car decks without disturbing the bridge? The bridge and crew cabins are right forward on that ship."

"The loading ramp is on the stern, but it closes up from inside and is clamped in place. If we had a cutting torch we could cut a hole in it." King Chu said.

"What about ventilators? Maybe we could drop down from above. The engines are aft, under the lower deck, but there is a big exhaust stack right up through all the car decks. Normally there are ladder rungs on the side of those things for maintenance. If we stay behind the stack, we wouldn't be visible from the bridge area. Of course, there could be cameras." Joe seemed to have a practical approach.

After some more discussion, we came up with what we thought was a workable plan. Billy arranged for Gina's jet to bring Aphrodite's crew to Vancouver for loading up.

I got Feinman to help me put together a tech kit for Saga. It consisted of a Delorme Inreach satellite communicator and a large external battery pack. The Delorme only allowed 160-character text messages each way, so Saga's capabilities would be greatly reduced on the ship. I wondered whether she would be useful at all.

In the end, I spent a couple of hours moving as much of the "brains" from the server to the phone as I possibly could. Only brief testing was possible, but Saga still seemed to work okay.

Charlie called me. I had almost forgotten about the charter boat.

"Hi Chan, bad news. I'm afraid I didn't find a suitable boat to charter. The fishing boats are too heavy and slow to catch that ship, and the faster boats I found are too small to carry what you will need. I do have an idea for you. There is a Grumman Albatross seaplane for sale in Dutch Harbor. It has been recently refurbished and has new turboprop engines. I spoke to the owner. Apparently, it can land and take off in the open sea. He is asking $450,000."

I wasn't prepared for this. I decided to hedge my bets. "Charter one of the slow fishing boats, including crew. Better tell them a week. Then offer the Albatross owner a hundred thousand for a 2-day charter, we'll pay for any damage, up to the full value. I'll get Saga to buy a couple of Zodiacs and a welding torch for delivery to the plane."

If all went to plan we'd be flying to Dutch Harbor the next day. I went back to my boat, poured myself a finger of Glen Fiddich, and got ready for bed.

# 15 I AM A JAPANESE WRITER

*I was in the corner of a four-mat room. The walls were Japanese paper screens. The center of the room had a low, black table with a lacquered gold dragon breathing painted fire in my direction. On the table were an iron teapot and two small, empty teacups. I looked across the table, and there was Gina. Her hair was up in Geisha style, and she wore a plain white kimono with a black obi. She was on her knees looking down at the teapot. I tried to call her name but no sound came out. I heard the swish of a sword through the air and all went black. I had a sensation of falling, falling, falling through the darkness.*

I awoke with a thump. I was in my bunk onboard Blue Rose. The early rays of the dawn sun were seeping through the portlights. I could hear water lapping against the hull. I got up, put the coffee on and talked to Saga.

"Saga, we have a big day ahead. You've been listening in and researching. Can you tell me what I have overlooked?"

"I have a list. Number one. The crew knows Gina and Tombolo are on board."

"How do you know that?"

"Elementary, my Dear Watson. There is no way that two people in a dinghy could board the Persephone without the crew's help. Therefore, I deduced that the crew knows about them. The satellite record showed that the ship slowed down to 6 knots for an hour, right about the time they would have reached her."

"That makes sense. So, we need to take that into

account. They might be looking out for an attack."

"I have intercepted some communications from the ship. It is encrypted, but I have partly cracked it. It is about preparations for offloading and guarding the cargo when they arrive in Tokyo. My conclusion is that they are expecting an attack there. I recommend that we leak some information that reinforces that. I suggest we book tickets to Tokyo for you, Billy and Joe, to arrive just before the Persephone. Then let detective Penrose know, and have her inform her counterparts in Tokyo that we are coming, and that she suspects we might try to organize a rescue."

"That sounds like a good red herring, but we better not let her know about our other plans. I'll call her now. You book the flights. Japan Air Lines if you can."

I got on the phone with Penrose and told her we planned to meet the ship in Japan. I asked her if she could arrange discreet Japanese police help. She agreed to try. I didn't mention Dutch Harbor or the high seas rescue at all.

Saga had more information for me.

"Number two. Captain Tanaka and his crew joined the Persephone in Vancouver. The previous crew flew home to Japan."

"Is that unusual?"

"I found a few similar instances, but in general, the same crew takes the return voyage."

"So, we might conclude that they are a hand-picked crew?"

"Probably, but there is more. Captain Tanaka's bank account in Japan received a large bank transfer from a corporate account in the Cayman Islands. The account belongs to a numbered company in the Bahamas. I traced that to a man named Kazuo Nimura. He is rumored to be a leader of Genyosha, a Japanese secret society. It was officially disbanded long ago but is believed by many to remain active, with no more than a dozen members. The published aim of the society was *'to honor the Imperial Family, respect the Empire and guard the rights of the people'* but in fact they were at times aligned with gangsters and right-wing extremists."

"Okay, I'm afraid I don't know very much Japanese history, and I don't have time to learn it now. Saga, how does that connect to Gina Lee? Has she done something to disrespect Japan or the Imperial family? I don't think she even knows she is part Japanese."

"I don't think Gina is the target. I think she is the bait, or maybe she is even part of the plot. I think the target is my software, and indirectly you. We threaten the secrecy of the Genyosha just by our existence."

"How would they know about us?"

"Your friends might have told someone, who told someone else. You even told Gina about me, although you didn't give enough information for her to understand my capabilities."

"If you're correct, we could be going into a trap. Do you have any ideas how to avoid it?"

"Yes. Don't go. Let Billy and the crew rescue Gina, if they can. You stay here, and think of ways to improve our security."

It was good advice. Very good advice. But, I couldn't help picturing Gina in chains, in a dungeon, maybe dying because I failed to rescue her. I knew it was crazy. I had only met her twice, and yet I cared deeply for her. I simply could not imagine a world in which she didn't exist. I started packing my bags for the trip to the airport.

# 16 FLIGHT OF DREAMS

Charlie picked me up in his SUV, and we headed for the private part of YVR. Gina's jet was parked in a corner, with other private jets. It was quite a bit bigger than most of them, about the size of a typical commuter plane.

I snapped a photo, "Saga, what kind of plane is that?"

"It is a Gulfstream V550. It has a range of 6500 nautical miles and a cruising speed of Mach 0.83. It carries a crew of two and up to twelve passengers."

She gave more specs, but I stopped listening as Billy came out to meet me. He showed me where to drop my bags and welcomed me aboard. I was introduced to the Pilot and Co-Pilot. Vicky, Curly and the rest of the crew were already on board. I had to fill them in on Saga's information.

"We are quite sure the ship's crew knows Gina and Tombolo are onboard. It is likely that we're heading into a trap. The ship's crew was newly boarded in Vancouver, so they are probably employed by the kidnappers. To me, that means they might be armed, or at least well prepared for us. If anybody wants to sit this one out, I wouldn't blame you. It could be deadly. Speak up now."

Nobody backed out, so the cargo door was closed and we all fastened seatbelts. The plane had four sections. The cockpit, with seats for the two crew, and a jump seat for an observer. Then there was the passenger cabin with eight seats, like a small airliner. Then there was Gina's private cabin with two sofas which could convert to beds and a satellite entertainment system with a large flat screen.

Before we took off, the pilot came back into the cabin. Captain Reynolds looked concerned. "When I filed my flight plan non-stop to Dutch Harbor, the information they gave me stated the runway is only 4100 feet long. This plane needs 5900 feet to take off, although we can land in under 3000 feet. So, we could land, but be unable to take off."

Not good. "Saga, is there another airport nearby with a longer runway?"

"Cold Bay has an airport with two runways, both over 6000 feet long. But it is 178 miles away from Dutch Harbor. There is an Alaska State ferry but it takes a long time with several stops."

"Can we get a pilot to fly the Albatross to Cold Bay and meet us there? We could fly directly to the ship from there."

"The Albatross can take off in only 1700 feet. It has a range of 2600 miles, so yes, that should be possible. I'll text Charlie to deal with this since I will lose communication in flight."

Captain Reynolds said, "Actually, we have Row 44 satellite-based Wi-Fi on board, so you will have high-speed internet in flight."

He didn't seem fazed by the talking phone. I guess people were getting so used to the technology they just accepted the resulting odd behavior.

"Excellent. Please re-file the flight plan for Cold Bay. How long will the flight take?"

"It will be less than four hours."

A US customs officer came on board to examine

our passports and pre-clear us for entry into the US. We told him we were on a hunting trip. Which was true.

In a few minutes, the plane was taxiing to the runway, and we were discussing our plan of action. After we were in the air, Curly served coffee and snacks. David used the internet on his tablet to bone up on the flying characteristics of the Grumman Albatross.

"Have you flown a seaplane before?" I asked him.

"Yes, I belong to an antique flying club. I have had a chance to fly a Catalina PBY a few times. I think the Grumman is a bit more modern if you can call a sixty-year-old plane modern."

Talk turned to weapons. I asked Saga about Alaska gun laws.

"According to Wikipedia, Alaska has the least restrictive gun laws in the US. You can buy handguns and rifles, even assault weapons, without a permit or waiting period. However, Cold Bay has a population of 88 and only one store. They probably don't have much stock."

"What about Dutch Harbor?"

"It is much bigger. There are two gun shops. A supermarket, an electronics store, and a large marine supply store. There are a few restaurants and cafes. I'll contact the gun stores and see what they have in stock."

Saga was showing initiative again. I didn't know whether to be pleased or frightened. I didn't remember specifically programming it.

Joe and King discussed their choice of weapons and declared the AR-15 rifle, if available, would be their choice. Billy wasn't a gun guy. Vicky preferred a Heckler & Koch G28 but doubted you could buy one in Dutch Harbor. I hadn't fired a gun since I was twelve, and that was a .22 rifle. I thought I'd take a small handgun, more for threatening than actual use.

While we waited for the gun inventory I nodded off in my seat.

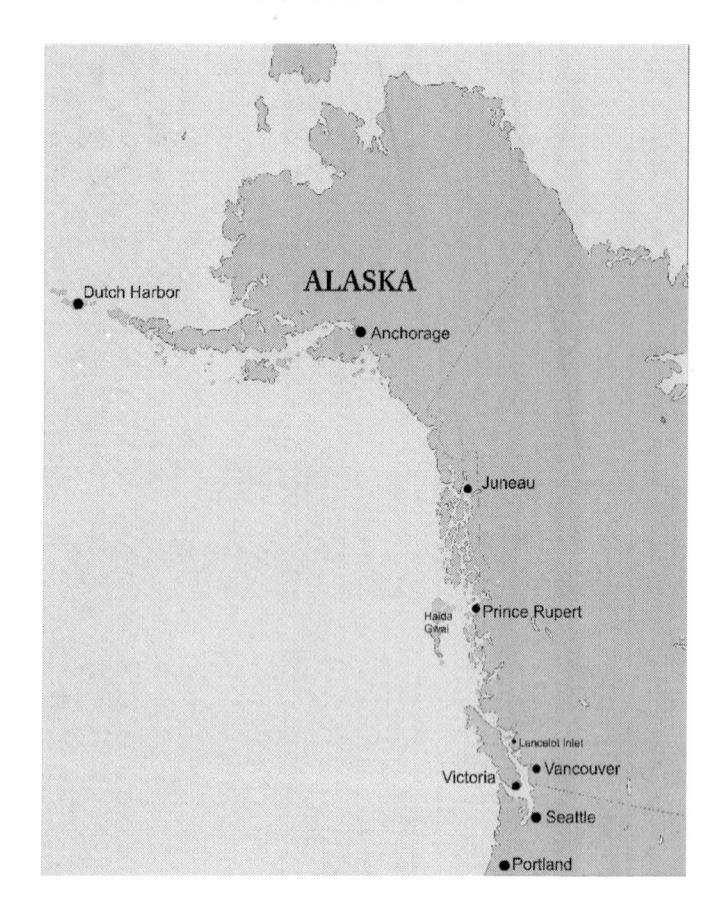

Map of Alaska and the BC Coast

# 17 ALL OUR HAPPY DAYS ARE STUPID

The bounce of the wheels on the rough tarmac of the Cold Bay airport woke me up. I was groggy, and it took me a few moments to realize where I was. The weather outside was gray, and rain streaked the windows. Cold Bay airport consisted of a single boxy two-story building, the two runways, and not much else. A couple of small private planes were parked on the edge of the runway, and we taxied over alongside them.

Captain Reynolds came out of the cockpit. "I just heard the tower talking to the Albatross, it should be here in about twenty minutes. Chan, while you were asleep we discussed how to handle the transition. There is not much here. We decided we'll fly with you to Dutch Harbor where there are a couple of hotels. We are all booked in at the Grand Aleutian, thanks to Saga."

"Wow, excellent. I didn't even think about where we would sleep and eat while we were there."

By the time we were unloaded we could see the seaplane coming in, wheels down. It landed easily in about a quarter of the length of the runway. While it was taxiing over I asked David if he was confident with flying the Albatross.

"I think I'll be okay. The incoming pilot can give me a quick lesson on the way back to Dutch Harbor. Apparently, the plane has a few quirks, but nothing scary. They can take off and land in up to four-foot waves, I hope it won't be rougher than that. The marine weather forecast for tomorrow says 15 knots of wind, three to five-foot seas."

The Albatross parked beside us and the engines shut down. It had about the same wingspan as the Gulfstream but was far bulkier looking. The props were huge. It was painted white on top and dark gray on the lower half. The wingtips and outriggers were yellow. It was an impressive looking craft. The pilot who climbed out the side door and down the steep ladder was impressive too.

He was not a tall man, but he was wide. His face was the color and texture of old leather boots, and he was completely bald except for a gray walrus mustache that would have made Hulk Hogan jealous. He was wearing jeans and a T-shirt, even though it was chilly and wet. His arms were densely tattooed in a style I didn't recognize.

He stuck out a massive hand as I stepped forward. "Jan Hermanson."

"Chandler Gray." Somehow I escaped his vice-like grip without any broken bones.

I introduced him to the rest of the crew and we started transferring our gear into the Albatross. It wasn't an easy job.

"Jan, how can we get a couple of Zodiacs with outboards in and out of the plane at sea? They won't fit through that small door."

"There is no way you could, on most of these planes, but look here." He took me around to the starboard side. There was a horizontal door about eight feet long and three high, with hinges at the top. "This plane was used for air-sea rescue, and they used to push an inflated life raft out that slot."

I climbed up the ladder and looked inside. It wasn't as roomy as I expected. I paced it off and concluded we could probably only fit one Zodiac on board. I had wanted two as a backup, but it didn't look possible.

"I guess we'll have to manage with just one dinghy. Is there a crane?"

Jan replied, "There is a small extendable crane with a manual crank. It can lift about 400 pounds."

"A 50 horsepower outboard weighs over 220 pounds, the dinghy would weigh that much again. And then there is the battery and fuel. I think we must forget about retrieving the dinghy."

My confidence in the whole mission was waning. Nothing was going exactly to plan.

Billy climbed into the plane. Sensing my mood, he clapped an arm around my shoulders. "Cheer up. We aren't defeated yet. We have a good team, and I'm sure we can make this work."

Somehow this made me feel better, and we got on with loading up. There were just enough seats for all of us if David sat in the co-pilot's seat. The other two pilots sat in the observer's seats behind them, and the rest of us strapped ourselves into military style jump seats which folded down along the sides of the fuselage. It certainly wasn't as comfortable as the Gulfstream, but at the same time, it was clearly built to military standards.

The turboprop engines were smooth and not as noisy as I expected. The plane taxied onto the runway and turned for takeoff. The plane rattled down the runway and lifted off in an amazingly short distance. Once airborne I looked out the side window. Cold Bay was on a small island, and I could see more steep green islands stretching in a chain into the distance. The Aleutians.

It took us almost two hours to get to Dutch Harbor. The Albatross cruises at just above a hundred, although it can do 200 in a pinch.

I could see why the runway was short. There was no room for a longer one. It stretched right across the island, with the ocean on both ends. The landing was smooth. Jan was a good pilot.

We taxied off the runway and parked on the verge. There were 3 Cessna-type planes and a middle-sized helicopter parked there.

David came out of the cockpit first. "What do you think? I landed her. She is not too hard to fly."

We all clapped.

"By the way, it turns out Jan owns the plane," added David.

"I wired him the money yesterday. Actually, I got Gina's lawyer to do it," Saga said.

Two mini-van taxis were there to pick us up. We planned to spend the night at the Grand Aleutian and load up in the morning. We dropped Jan off at his house—a mobile home—and continued on to the Grand Aleutian

It was an attractive European style hotel with a restaurant and a couple of bars. There were plenty of rooms so we each got one. Wi-Fi was available but cost extra. We agreed to meet for dinner at six and review the plan for the next day.

I asked Saga when the Persephone would pass closest to Dutch Harbor.

"Based on her present course and speed, she will be about one hundred fifteen miles away at 2 AM Saturday."

It was Thursday afternoon. We would have all day Friday to get our equipment together and loaded on the plane.

We met for dinner in the Chart Room. The menu was mostly seafood, as you might have expected. They had a great selection of beer, I ordered a Bleeding-Heart Brew and the Alaskan King Crab.

While we waited for the food, I updated the schedule.

"Saga says the Persephone will be at her closest at two AM Saturday. It would be about an hour flying time from here."

David said, "The airport control tower will be closed then, and the runway lights will be off. I suggest we take off from the harbor. I'd like to try a couple of landings on the water anyway. Jan has offered to go up with me tomorrow,"

"Good idea. It looks to me as if we can only take one Zodiac on the plane. Saga, what is the capacity of the boats you bought?"

"FedEx couldn't deliver a rigid floor Zodiac here. I ended up with two twelve foot Saturn dinghies because they had the biggest air floor model. They are rated at 5 persons or 1433 pounds of total cargo. I also got two BF-20 Honda outboards which should give over twenty knots. I chose them because they are the most powerful motors with hand start. The total weight of the dinghy, motor and fuel is less than 300 pounds. The dinghy shipping box will fit through the door of the plane."

"Wow. Good work. We'll be able to take two dinghies, but we'll only have room to inflate one in the plane."

"The gun shop has AR-15s but not the Heckler

and Koch. Sorry Vicky."

"That's okay, Saga." They sounded like buddies. I wondered when and how that happened.

"I reserved a nine-millimeter Sig-Sauer pistol for you, Chan. They have plenty of ammunition in stock. The dinghies and the line launchers are waiting at the Marine Supply store. The taxi company has a big panel van we can use to move it all to the plane."

I was impressed. "Excellent work Saga. I'm thinking we'll use only one dinghy. Vicky will drive it and remain with it until we come back. Billy and David will stay on board the plane to help load and unload the equipment. Curly, I'd like you to stay here at the hotel just in case we need to be rescued. We'll text you updates as we go. That leaves me, Joe and King as the boarding party. There will be room in the dinghy for Gina. I don't plan to bring anyone else back with us."

Joe said, "We'll need restraints and gags. Zip strips work well and every hardware store has them."

"I brought all of that, including ball gags, in my luggage. I brought a bottle of chloroform too. I don't want to kill or maim anyone if at all possible," I said.

After dinner, we discussed the actual deployment of the dinghy and boarding the ship. We decided to try a practice run the next day. Breakfast would be at 8 AM then we would get the weapons and other equipment to load the plane. We went to our rooms early to get a good night's sleep.

I turned on the TV Weather Channel but there didn't seem to be much information for that remote area. I got Saga to get the marine weather from

NOAA over the internet. It predicted west winds at twelve to sixteen knots and seas of three to five feet.

I started watching Hawaii Five-O. I was amused by the unlikely level of violence, but I supposed that was what sold. A few minutes in there was a knock at the door. It was Vicky. She was wearing flannel pajamas which failed to hide her formidable physique.

"Uh, Vicky, this is inappropriate."

She looked past me. "What are you talking about? I'm here to see Saga."

Vicky brushed past me and stood by the window.

"Saga, I'm afraid I have been a bad girl."

Saga replied in her most British accent. "Well, slave, I suppose you will have to be punished."

I decided I didn't need to hear more and slipped out into the hall. I went downstairs and picked up a brochure about the local museum. From that I learned that Dutch Harbor had been bombed by the Japanese Navy in 1942. I had the weird thought that by attacking a Japanese ship we were somehow retaliating for the attack. I knew there was no connection but the thought persisted.

I strolled into the Cape Cheerful Lounge. To my surprise, it was quite lively, with a small and not too loud band playing. The crowd seemed to be a mixture of locals and tourists. Jan was there, and he motioned me over to his table and bought me a Corona. After about an hour of general chitchat about hunting, fishing, and football—all of which I knew nothing about—I took my leave and went back up to the room. I passed Vicky in the hall but she ignored me. And so, to bed.

## 18 I HAVE NO MOUTH AND I MUST SCREAM

*The room was circular, bright, with a featureless white wall and domed ceiling. The floor was polished teak, with a single Bokhara rug in the center, and a few large leather cushions spread around in random fashion. I was standing on one side of the room, with no idea how I got there. The only opening in the wall was deeply recessed, and I couldn't see into it from my position. I was alone. I walked over to the opening, which had a circular window at the end of a short hallway. Outside it was blue-green with waving weeds and sand. A fish swam by and I realized I was on the bottom of the sea. A large shark swam rapidly toward the window and I took a step back. He opened his jaws wide as he neared the glass.*

*Gina's face looked out from his open mouth. She was smiling happily.*

I woke with a start. "Your Mother is calling." said the phone in Saga's British voice.

I sent it to voicemail.

After breakfast, we went to the gun shop Saga had selected. It was a big place with glass counters in rows, and pegboard walls with a variety of weapons. What surprised me was that only a few of the weapons seemed to be hunting rifles. There were a lot that looked like combat weapons, even though as far as I knew there was no war on.

The staff consisted of three burly men who looked like bikers, but they were polite and friendly. Ben, the guy who served us told me that the majority of the weapons were for hunting, but "combat styling" was popular.

We collected three AR-15s and a variety of clips and ammunition. I found the Sig-Sauer comfortable in hand and Ben took me out back and let me test fire it. He handed me a set of ear protectors. It was loud and kicked more than I had expected. It worked best held two-handed. In a few minutes, I was confident I could hit a large stationary target at short range. Ben recommended a shoulder holster for it, and I bought it.

Joe and King were swinging their AR-15s around, aiming them at each other and generally horsing about. Billy spoke to them quietly and they started packing up.

Billy put the whole thing on his credit card, and we loaded up the taxi van for a trip to the Albatross. Saga was quiet.

Soon we had the van unloaded and Billy, Joe, and King went off to get the dinghies and outboards, along with the line launchers. I was beginning to think we might succeed.

Vicky, Curly and I stowed the weapons on board the Albatross while David looked over the controls, checked the air in the tires and made sure all the fluids were topped up.

"What could possibly go wrong?" I mumbled to myself. I meant it rhetorically but Saga answered.

"You could shoot yourself in the foot. The plane could crash. The dinghy could capsize. You might not be able to get on board Persephone. They might fight back and kill you all."

"So, nothing serious then. I'll just concentrate on

the job at hand. Can you verify the position and course of the ship, and check the weather again?"

"Si, El Jefe." She sounded like Speedy Gonzales. I wondered if her cultural references were age specific? I was sure a Millennial wouldn't get that one. I know I wrote the software, but the machine learning code I put in seemed to have some unexpected capabilities. I hoped they were useful for something else besides making fun of me.

By the time we got everything tied down, the crew was back with the dinghies. We decided to inflate one on the runway, then try to load it on board the plane. It was a good thing we did.

"This damn foot pump is too slow. It will take ages to get this inflated," Joe grumbled. It was true. It was a big dinghy but the pump was the same one you would use for a seven-footer.

"I'll go to the marine store and see if they have an electric pump," Billy said. I volunteered to accompany him in case I thought of anything else.

Dutch Harbor isn't very big, so it didn't take long to get there. On the way, I remembered the fishing boat we had supposedly chartered. I called Charlie and got the name and number of the captain. I brought Charlie up to speed in a very general way, without mentioning any names or locations. I made it sound like a fishing trip.

The fishing boat was called Her Ring II. I was sure there was a story behind the name, but that would have to wait. The Captain was one Don Spitzley. I called him up.

"Spitzley."

"Chandler Gray. I'm part of the group that has chartered your boat for the next few days."

"Yeah? I was wondering when you would show up."

"What I'd like you to do is go to a location about 100 miles out and wait for us. We'll be coming out that way by plane. We want you to stand by in case we need rescuing, which is quite likely."

"What the hell kind of crap is this? Ain't you even coming with us?"

"No, but there is a chance we'll be returning with you later. Did we wire you enough to cover it?"

"Yeah. All right. It will take us about ten hours to get out there. What time do you want to meet up?"

"About 2 AM tomorrow. Please monitor VHF channel 69, we'll call you when we are nearby." The standard calling channel is sixteen, but Persephone would be listening on that one too, so I didn't want to chance it.

Those arrangements complete, I followed Billy into Alaska Ship Supply. It was really a big general store and even had a coffee shop. The marine department wasn't huge, but we found a powerful electric air pump. I also thought to buy three floating handheld VHF walkies, inflatable life jackets and strobe lights for all of us, and four black hoodies, which had the store's logo on them. It was all they had. They seemed familiar looking. A small sign said, "As seen on Deadliest Catch". I hoped that wasn't an omen.

We loaded up the van and I bought some coffees for everyone.

When we got back to the plane, the dinghy was half inflated, but the crew was busy unpacking the outboards. The electric pump made short work of the remaining inflation. Then we tried to hoist it up through the slot in the side of the plane. It didn't fit. When the crane was deployed, there wasn't enough room to get the boat and outboard through. It would go through with the crane retracted, but then we couldn't lift it from inside.

"It looks like we'll have to deflate it, load it up the ladder, then inflate it inside the plane. When we come back to the plane, we'll have to abandon the dinghy. Maybe the fishing boat can pick it up," Joe said.

We all nodded and King let the air out. It was comical trying to roll it up small enough to get it back in the bag it came with. Eventually, we got it loaded and inflated inside. It would go through the slot, but not with the outboard attached. In the end, we lashed the motor on the floor of the dinghy. It weighed over 100 pounds so moving it to the transom would be a chore.

Once loaded up, Billy and I went back to the hotel, leaving David and the rest of the crew to fly the plane to a mooring in the bay. David planned to make a few takeoff and landing passes to get used to ungainly looking plane.

Once back at the hotel, we sat down to finalize our strategy. Billy talked first.

"David suggested we fly in high, as marine radar is aimed low to pick up other ships and land, not planes. Then we dive down rapidly and land in the wake of the ship. He will keep the motors running and match the speed of Persephone, staying close enough to be under the ships radar. I have never noticed airplanes showing on Afro's radar. The wheelhouse is right forward on that ship, and the antennas are on top of it, so there is a large blind spot behind the ship. Of course, they may have a rear facing camera, but they wouldn't be keeping a close watch on that."

"Okay, that should work. Then we deploy the dinghy, and the four of us get on board and start the motor. I hope the line launchers and rope ladders work," I said.

"Have you ever climbed a rope ladder?"

"Only a short one to board a yacht after swimming."

"A fifty-foot ladder might move around a lot."

"I suppose. I was once on a sea trial on an icebreaker in big seas. It had metal ladders between decks. The trick was to climb when it was heading down, and just hang on when it was moving up."

"That would work, but what about a rolling motion?"

"I guess we'll find out. Since the wheelhouse is forward, and there are only two doors out of it to the deck, we could jam those to lock in the crew, or just ignore them and hope they don't notice us."

"The engine room is aft, and the ship's engineer might be in there. We'll have to play some of it by ear. I brought six long range headset radios so we can all talk without shouting and a can of black spray paint on an extender for surveillance cameras."

Billy had thought of quite a few things I missed. A good man.

Later the crew came back and we had dinner together in the hotel. David told us about the test flights.

"I was surprised how well that old bird flies. The turboprops are more powerful than the original engines, and she just jumps off the runway. The landing gear retracts unevenly, one side then the other, and you must compensate with the throttles. Taking off from water needs more distance but she still lifts off fast. Landings are fairly easy. They recently fitted a camera low down on the bow so you can see how far off the water you are. It helps a lot."

"There is no water rudder, but the props reverse, so you can spin it on the spot. Moving fast you can steer with the air rudder. It is an excellent plane."

We were all pleased to hear that, as our lives depended on it. After dinner, we went to the lounge to unwind.

The place was crowded again that evening, it was some sort of open mike night. After a huge Samoan dude in a black wife-beater sang an amazing off-key version of My Way, Vicky stepped up wearing a white t-shirt with Aphrodite written across her impressive breasts. Applause all round. I took note that men outnumbered women about ten to one.

"This is my little friend Dick. He is the world's funniest robot. So, slap your digits together for little Dick."

Vicky held up a shoebox with a collar and tie scrawled on the front in felt pen. There was a pair of baby shoes duct taped to one end. The head was an inflated condom with a smiley face on it. She moved it close to the mike.

## TIGER AND THE ROBOT

*Good evening Smartphones, droids, and your mammalian carriers. Have you ever noticed how bad they smell? No? That's because you don't have advanced molecular vapor sensors like I do.*

*It was a robotic sounding male voice. I was sure it was Saga. But my phone was in my pocket. I suppose she could be using Skype to talk through Vicky's phone.*

*A primitive robot was programmed by a CIA programmer to detect lies. It would deliver an electric shock as soon as it detected a lie. Not wanting to show it off at work without testing it, he took it home and tried it on his family.*

*When Johnny came home late that evening his father asked him where he had been.*

*"I was at Pete's studying." The Robot shocked him.*

*"The robot gives you a shock if you lie." His father explained.*

*"Okay, we watched a movie on Netflix." The robot shocked Johnny again.*

*"Okay, we watched porn."*

*"Johnny, when I was your age, I didn't know what porn was!" The robot shocked him.*

*His mother laughed. 'He's definitely your son!" The robot shocked her.*

*He took the robot back to work, but it was never deployed because it kept shocking the director of the CIA.*

The audience loved it. There was more, including jokes about people in the crowd. I wondered how Saga could see them, but I remembered I was wearing the camera glasses. By then it was a habit.

*When I was just a baby robot, I thought my master was a*

*god. Later, I thought he was a great scientist. Now I know he's just a big Dick.*

That ended the evening for me. That last joke wasn't funny. I went back to my room and tried to get some sleep before our middle of the night departure.

## 19 UNDER THE JOLLY ROGER

Saga woke me up by playing *Anchors Aweigh*. It was one AM. I dragged myself to the bathroom and splashed cold water on my face. Saga still couldn't make coffee, but I made some Nescafe with the pot provided.

I was the first one downstairs, but the rest were there in short order and we piled into the van. Nobody looked too lively, but what could you expect at that hour. Billy brought a crash kit with duct tape, wire, an EPIRB *(Emergency Position Indicating Radio Beacon)* and other goodies. I felt we were as well prepared and equipped as possible. I refrained from asking Saga what could go wrong.

The plane was on a mooring. There was an old runabout belonging to Jan which we used to get ourselves on board. We left it on the mooring for our return. Saga gave David the coordinates where she estimated the ship would be at 2 AM and he entered a waypoint in the GPS.

Billy sat in the co-pilot's seat beside David. Apparently, he had flying lessons long ago, although he didn't have a license. Vicky and I sat behind David in the observer's seats. Once the motors spun over and the turbines began to whine it was too loud for conversation. The sky had cleared and the moon was nearly full, so visibility was good.

David ran up the engines, and Joe let go the mooring line. We taxied out to the edge of the harbor, then turned to face the island, into the wind. Once lined up he jammed the throttles forward. The

Albatross pushed water for a few seconds then jumped up on plane like a fast power boat. After a couple of gentle bounces, we were airborne and climbing. The view was stunning. The Aleutian chain is mountainous, and the islands stretched off into the distance in shades of blue-gray, like a Tony Onley painting. A few white patches on the peaks revealed unmelted snow. The moon left a shining path on the water.

We leveled out at about 5000 feet, high enough to be above marine radar but low enough to spot the ship when we got close. I just enjoyed the view, aware that I might never see it, or any other view again.

While we were flying, Billy came back and opened the crash bag, taking out what looked like an ordinary digital camera, but with a handle extending out the bottom. "This is a Flir K65 Thermal Imager. It shows a heat image. It can detect the warmth of a human body, and the heat signature where one has been for several minutes."

He showed me how to operate it and I practiced by looking around the plane. It showed colors ranging from blue for cold though yellow and orange as the temperature increased. Like a regular camera, it automatically adjusted the exposure. When I aimed it out the windows I could clearly see the heat pattern of the engines. I turned it off and tucked it back in the crash bag.

"Thanks, Billy. I can see how that could be useful."

About an hour later Billy pointed to the GPS which indicated we were getting close to the waypoint. David banked the plane in a large arc so we could look down at the water. We could still see the Aleutians off to one side, but there was no sign of the ship.

"Saga, can you update the location of the ship?" I spoke into my pocket. The reply took at least a minute. The Delorme satellite modem was very slow.

"The ship is now about six miles south of the position I gave you before. They must have changed course since we left." She spoke slowly in a robotic voice. The main speech engine was on the server so she couldn't use it.

I leaned forward and relayed this to David. He banked the plane to a southerly heading and we soon spotted the ship, or at least her wake, which seem to glow in the dark. It was a few miles ahead of us on almost the same course.

I took out a portable VHF and called on channel 69.

"Her Ring, Her Ring, this is Albatross."

There was a brief pause, and just as I was about to try again the radio crackled. "This is Herring. We can see the ship on radar, we're about seven miles away. Where are you?"

"We're dead aft of her. Please set a course across Persephone's stern on a diagonal so it doesn't look as if you're chasing her. I'll call again when we are done. If you don't hear from me within an hour, call us."

"Roger that. Herring out."

David cut the throttles part way and went into a steep dive, banking to place us at right angles to the ship's course. That way if we were spotted on radar it would look like we were heading away. In a couple of minutes, the sea was coming up fast and David leveled off smoothly, only about fifty feet above the waves. He adjusted the throttles until we were cruising at about 70 knots. When he was in a direct line with the ships course and about a mile behind, he cut the power completely and we dropped into the ships wake. The landing was rough but not damaging. Then we were in boat mode. The waves were not huge but we still pitched and rolled some.

More throttle was needed to match the ship's speed, and we inched forward until we were about 500 feet away. Then David feathered the props and brought us to a halt. He shut down the engines. The plane slowly rotated into the wind.

"Get that dinghy launched before the ship gets too far away," Billy commanded.

Joe and King opened the side door and pushed the dinghy out. Vicky took the bow line and I took the stern line. The drop to the water was only about three feet, and the boat hit with a splash. Without hesitation Joe and King jumped in and unlashed the motor from the floor, hefting it onto the transom. For a moment, it looked like they would lose it, but Joe grabbed it and held on while King tightened the clamps. Then they hooked up the fuel tank.

Billy took the bow line from Vicky, and she jumped in. She went to the Honda, pumped the primer bulb then pulled the cord. The first pull was too slow and it didn't start. She put her back into it and the motor revved and died. After three more pulls it started and ran smoothly.

I tied off the stern line and started tossing the

weapons and other equipment to King, and Joe lashed them down. It was no more than five minutes since we opened the door but the ship had moved quite a distance away. I untied the stern line, tossed it to Joe and jumped aboard.

Billy threw the bow line to King and we were off. Vicky backed us away from the stationary props of the Albatross, then gunned the motor. The boat was heavily loaded but the motor was strong and soon we were moving a little faster than the ship. It took us about ten minutes to catch up to the Persephone. On the way, Joe readied the line launcher and attached a grappling hook to the line.

As we approached the ship we could see that it had a large door in the transom, hinged at the bottom, obviously the loading ramp for cars and trucks. The deck was at least 60 feet off the water, surrounded by sturdy looking pipe guardrails. Joe kneeled in the bottom of the boat. He signaled Vicky to match the ships speed and aimed the gun as we bounced a bit in the ships wake,

He fired. The gun made a loud pneumatic bang and the line snaked out. The grappling hook hit the transom just below the deck and bounced off into the sea. Joe retrieved the line and started reloading the gun to fire again.

"Wi-Fi access obtained." Saga spoke from my pocket. "Unsecured. No password needed."

"Shit!"

Joe cursed as he dropped the compressed air cartridge. King picked it up from the floor and handed back to him. He screwed it in place and started to aim again.

Suddenly a loud creaking noise started above us. "I have obtained control of the ramp motors. The whole ship is networked. Opening ramp door."

"Won't that alert the crew?" I imagined a flashing red light and a siren whooping, as portrayed in a Bond film.

"No, I have also disabled the warning notifications."

"Saga is opening the ramp," I shouted because I didn't think they could hear her. Actually, her voice was already coming through the headsets we all wore and there was no need to shout. She was also speaking in her normal voice and British accent, so I guessed she was connected to her server through the ship's satellite connection.

The ramp slowly lowered. Joe picked up his AR-15 and aimed it at the opening. Vicky backed us off until it was all the way down, about three feet off the water. There were cleats on the corners and welded steps up one side. Vicky gunned the motor and King leaped athletically onto the ramp with the bow line. In seconds, we were tied up, and Vicky cut the power, letting the ship tow us. The ramp was hanging down at about a 30-degree angle, and we couldn't see into the ship.

"Wait," I said. "Let Saga take a look with her drone."

I got the drone out of its waterproof bag and switched it on. Saga took control and flew it into the cargo bay of the huge ship. I took the phone out and watched the screen. There were footlights on around the periphery of the deck. As the drone flew down the center aisle of the main car deck the camera swiveled left and right, but there were no signs of life. There were no vehicles at all on that deck.

"Saga, this ship has 5 vehicle decks. The one you're on is the second from the bottom. They would put heavy vehicles on the lowest deck, I imagine that's where the motor home will be."

She turned the drone around and flew to a stairwell, then carefully maneuvered it down the steps and into the bottom deck. The camera showed three large vehicles and a slightly smaller one which was the motor home. It was in the middle lane, about half way forward. A power cord was connected to it from an outlet on a stanchion nearby. There were no lights on in the motorhome, not surprising since it was the middle of the night.

I grabbed the crash bag and clambered onto the ramp. Joe and King had their guns ready and we moved quietly forward to the ramp the drone went down. It made sense to go the same way since the drone hadn't encountered anyone. I was a bit puzzled by this, but maybe our false trail to Tokyo had worked.

The lower deck was dimly lit. We approached the motorhome quietly. I signaled Joe and King to standby as I got out the infrared camera and switched it on. I scanned the motorhome with it. The temperature was a pretty uniform blue except for three rectangular areas which showed yellow. I assumed those were the batteries and the charger. I put the camera away and tried the door. It was unlocked. I opened it slowly. It was a new vehicle and the hinges were quiet. I waved Joe aboard, and he switched on a small LED flashlight. He had his gun ready. I could see his shadow moving through the cabin, and I followed him in, leaving King to stand guard.

"Nobody here." Joe's voice came through my headset.

I opened the fridge. Empty. It looked like our guess about where Gina would be kept was wrong.

"They must be in the crew accommodation." I unfolded a sketch I had made from the ships plans. "There are three decks in the superstructure. The top one is the bridge, and the Captain's cabin is located on that level, as is the First Mate's. The middle deck has the galley, dining room, TV lounge and gym. The crew cabins are on the bottom deck."

Joe spoke quietly. "If they are unarmed, we could storm the place and tie them up pretty fast. But if they are armed, and there are fifteen of them, we don't stand a chance."

"How about if Saga flies her drone around the outside and looks in the windows? That and the infrared camera might help us figure out where they are. Maybe if Gina is being held in the crew area, we could free her without alerting the bridge."

"It's worth a try. We should carry the drone up there by hand, to save the batteries."

Saga had landed the drone beside the motorhome, and I picked it up. We went back to the stairwell we had come down. Then we climbed the stairs as quietly as possible. The sound of the ships engine, ventilation fans, and other ship noises drowned out our footfalls.

When we got to the top there was a watertight steel door to the deck. You had to unscrew a wheel to release the latches. It squeaked loudly when King turned it, and I wished I had a can of WD-40. We waited a minute after he opened it a crack, but there was no activity on deck, so we stepped out.

The decks were light gray and the upper works were white, clearly visible in the moonlight. We were about fifty feet aft of the superstructure. There were lights on in the middle decks, and a dim red glow came from the bridge, which made sense. Red light doesn't destroy night vision, so it was used for the footlights and instruments.

We moved along the inside of the port bulwark, which was in shadow. When we were alongside the house, I got out the drone.

"Saga, can you fly past the bridge first, and see how many people are up there. I would expect at least two. Don't fly directly in front, just go by the side windows quickly and the drone probably won't be spotted. Then fly by the windows that have lights on. Since there are no lights on the bottom I'm assuming anyone down there is asleep."

I watched the phone screen, but she flew too quickly for me to be able to follow. Saga gave me a running commentary.

"Nobody on the bridge. Portside I can see into the galley. Pots on the stove. No people. Dining area empty. Gym dark. Lounge lights on, no people."

"Okay, bring the drone back down. We might need it again." The drone had only enough battery for about ten minutes flying.

I got out the infrared camera and played it across the deckhouse. It showed pipes and ducts and other shapes, but nothing resembling a person. I wasn't sure they would show through the steel skin of the house. I opened a door to the crew cabins on the bottom, Joe covering me, and aimed the camera down the hallway. Nothing.

Feeling braver I stepped up to one of the cabin doors and knocked. Joe was ready for anyone that came out. Nothing. I opened the door and looked in. There was a bed, a dresser, a TV and some books. No people.

We repeated the same procedure at each cabin, moving faster as we began to suspect they were all empty. They were.

"This could be a trap," Joe said what I was thinking.

"Yes. If we go up to the next floor, they could lock the door behind us, and if all of them are somehow hidden up there they could overpower us easily."

Saga said, "I'm 90% sure there is nobody on board. I have been monitoring the network activity and have determined that the ship is being remotely controlled through the satellite link. The ship is sending the radar image and one bow mounted camera image as well as the GPS position to the satellite. I have recorded the IP that is controlling it so I can trace it later. This isn't a secure connection for that work."

We quickly went through the rest of the deckhouse. Saga was right. There was no sign of anyone on board, although beds looked slept in, and there was food in the fridge and even soup simmering in the galley. A modern-day Mary Celeste. There was also no sign that Gina or Tombolo had ever been there.

"They must have known we were coming and abandoned ship as a defensive measure. I'm sure they are nearby and will come back soon," Joe said.

"But how?" King asked

"Saga, there is a helicopter pad on the deck. Do the satellite photos show a helicopter on board?" I should have thought of this before.

"Yes, a fairly large one. I only get one photo a day, but the last one shows the chopper in place."

"Okay, we know how they got off, and maybe why, but not where they went to."

"Dutch Harbor is the nearest airport, but a chopper could land on any of these islands."

I was devastated. Another wild herring, or was it a red goose? Whoever we were dealing with was playing games with us. Successfully. I remembered something else from the museum brochure. When the Allies sent 35,000 US and Canadian troops to liberate Kiska Island in 1943, no Japanese were found. They had escaped under cover of a heavy fog.

They had done it to us too. But it wasn't foggy.

I packed up the drone. "Let's go. Maybe we can catch up to the chopper and question the crew."

The wind had picked up and the ship had developed a long slow roll. I took out the VHF and called Billy.

"Albatross, Albatross, this is CG. Over."

"CG, Albatross here. What is your situation?" It was Billy's voice.

"Nothing here. Returning to base. Watch for us."

I packed up the drone and the camera and we sprinted for the stairs. We got down as quickly as we could onto the stern ramp. Vicky and the dinghy were gone. The line was still on the cleat, but it had been cut, leaving a three-foot tail.

I cupped my mouth with my hands and shouted into the wind, "Vicky where are you?"

"Right here." Her voice was in my headset. I could hear the outboard and the dinghy came speeding into view moments later. "It got rougher and the line was jerking, so I cut myself loose."

While we were boarding the dinghy, several bigger waves washed up the ramp and entered the card deck of the ship. Vicky skillfully kept the bow in place while King jumped in first. One at a time Joe tossed him the weapons and the crash bag which he caught and lowered to the floor smoothly. Then Joe handed me off to King and jumped in himself. Vicky backed off the throttle and the ship pulled away. Then she gunned it and swung around into the wake.

It was a wet, bouncy fifteen-minute ride and we had to hang on to the rope handholds on the gunwale. The first cold water in the face was shocking but after that I was numb. We could see the plane ahead when David switched on the landing lights. He shut down the motors for safety and let it weathercock in the waves, with the port side—the one with boarding ladder—towards us.

When we got alongside King threw the bow line to Billy who caught and secured it in one smooth sweep of his arm. I should have been impressed but my mind was elsewhere. Vicky cut the motor and shut off the fuel. We prepared to abandon the boat. I climbed onboard first and caught the gear that Joe tossed up. Vicky boarded next, and then the others. Billy untied the line and tossed it into the dinghy. It didn't blow away, as the plane drifting down on it pinned it in place. David started the engines, and as soon as the port prop sent a blast of air back, the dinghy blew off.

Billy pulled up the ladder and secured the door. Then he called the Herring on the VHF and told them the position of the dinghy. He told them they could keep it if they picked it up, and then head back to port. His voice sounded angry.

The plane was now moving slowly into the wind and waves. We all went to our seats and strapped ourselves in.

David opened the throttles partway, and we sped up, but before we got going too fast, the crashing of the waves against the aluminum hull was so violent he backed off the throttles.

"It's too rough to take off. We'll have to taxi back. It could take eight or ten hours."

Billy said, "The waves aren't all the same size, wait for a lull and try again."

"Okay, but I have my doubts..." David said.

In a few minutes, the waves seemed smaller and David gunned the engines. The plane leaped forward and bounced violently, but kept accelerating. Spray flew high into the air as the pontoon outside my window hit each wave. Then it quieted down for a moment. We were airborne just above the waves.

Suddenly the front of the plane rose and we seem to slide backward. The plane fell into the rough water with a huge crash. I could hear metal tearing and the others screaming. Something hit the back of my head...

When I opened my eyes, Vicky was unfastening my seatbelt. The lights were still on. She saw I was awake and handed me an inflatable life vest. While I struggled with it, Joe and King were frantically trying to blow up the second dinghy. Both the electric pump and the foot pump were in use.

Billy found the foot pump from the other dinghy and connected it. He started pumping too. The outer tubes had three compartments. When the bow compartment filled with air Joe moved the electric pump to the one Billy was working on.

The engines were dead and the plane was wallowing. Vicky dragged David out of the pilot's seat. He had a cut on his forehead and she wiped the blood off with a towel. His eyelids fluttered. He was conscious but not mobile.

We loaded David and Vicky along with the outboard in the floor of the dinghy. There was water around our ankles as Joe opened the side door. Cold water sloshed in. Joe, King and I pushed hard against the incoming waves and got the dinghy out. Water poured in. The lights flickered and went out.

Billy shouted. "Everybody out! Inflate vests as soon as you're clear."

The plane listed so the door was submerged. I dove into the water, which was visibly brighter than the inside of the Albatross. Something grabbed my ankle and held on. Fear wrenched my guts. The plane was sinking, and I would go down with it. By instinct, I reached for the Wichard sailing knife on my belt. It wasn't there. Airport security.

# TIGER AND THE ROBOT

Something hit my forehead.

My father was holding me up with one hand under my belly. "Kick, kick. Stroke your arms like pulling the water toward you."

I kicked my feet and tried to pull the warm, clear tropical water toward me. He took his hand away. I started to sink and suddenly the water was black and cold. Ahead of me, a small intense white light shone through the gloom. Somehow, I knew that this was death, and death was my friend. I swam toward the light.

"There he is." Vicky's muffled voice seemed to come from the light. I kicked hard and my sea-boot came off, freeing me. I kicked off the other boot and swam upward toward the light. The water was cold but when I broke the surface the air seemed even colder.

The dinghy was only about ten feet away still tied to the plane. Vicky was in the bow with a knife, ready to cut the line as the plane went under. Billy was hanging on to the ropes looped along the side, unable to climb aboard. Joe was a few feet away, swimming strongly. When he got to the boat he rolled over the tube effortlessly and stood up to help Billy.

"Where's King?" Vicky shouted.

A hand waved from the far side of the dinghy and King rolled aboard just like Joe. The two of them each grabbed one of Billy's arms and hoisted. Then I was the only one left in the water. My eyes were drooping, and I was moving slowly, like swimming through molasses. I heard the outboard start. It sounded far off, but moments later strong arms dragged me into the boat. I lay exhausted on the floor beside David.

Vicky had one of the portable VHF radios in her hand. I sat up.

"Mayday, Mayday. Albatross calling Herring."

Nothing. After about a minute, she repeated the same thing. We were about fifty feet from the plane. It was almost on its side, with the starboard wing completely submerged. There was a cracking sound and the windshield exploded outward. Air rushed out and water rushed in. It was probably less than a minute until the plane disappeared beneath the waves, leaving disturbed water and huge bubbles erupting from below.

Finally, the VHF crackled. "Albatross, this is Herring. What is the situation?"

"The plane crashed. We are all in the dinghy, two injured. Over." Vicky was surprisingly calm.

"Can you give us a position? Over."

The VHF radios I bought had a built-in GPS. I was silently thankful. Vicky read out the position. There was a pause which seemed forever but was probably only a couple of minutes.

"Albatross, this is Herring. We are about seven miles away, steaming full speed toward you. Call me when you see us, we'll have our fishing lights on."

"Roger that. Albatross out."

Billy had a crash bag, and he handed out aluminum reflective blankets. I spread one over David and wrapped one around myself. Lying on the floor we were at least out of the wind. The other four huddled together in front of the transom.

The white tops of the waves glowed in the darkness as they rolled under the boat. Every few minutes a bigger wave would splash us with cold, salt spray. Joe bailed with his hat. Nobody said anything for about forty minutes. Then King shouted out. "There they are!"

I sat up again. He pointed toward the northwest, where we could see the bright lights of the fishing boat. Vicky hailed them on the radio and gave our latest position. Five minutes passed before they were alongside us to leeward. Vicky started the motor and powered us around to the other, more sheltered side. Joe and King carried David to the rail where two burly fishermen took him aboard. Then they helped me over the rail.

The cabin was warm, and there was hot coffee. The crew loaned us dry clothes, which were too big for any of us. Nobody cared. It was a ten-hour trip back to Dutch harbor, and I slept most of the way. I dreamt of Japanese pirates and flaming junks being attacked by kamikazes.

I woke as the edge of the rising sun painted a golden glow on the horizon. A few hours later we arrived safely in Dutch Harbor. David had recovered and was cheerfully joking with the crew of the Herring.

## 20 THIS CHANGES EVERYTHING

As soon as we landed, Billy told me he wanted to talk to me alone. We called a cab, and the rest of the crew waited for a mini-van.

Billy said nothing on the short cab ride, but he didn't look happy. When we got out he told me to meet him in the lounge in ten minutes. I went up to my room, showered quickly and dressed in Chinos, a blue collared shirt, and Topsiders. My regular uniform. I installed Saga's app in my spare phone, then headed down. I didn't know what to expect.

He was already there when I arrived. As soon as I sat at the table he leaned forward. He spoke softly but menacingly.

"Gray, you're a damned fool. This is the second wild goose chase you've led us on, with the same result. Nothing. This time it was dangerous, we crashed an expensive, uninsured plane, and it is just blind luck nobody was killed."

I opened my mouth to speak, but he held up his palm. I shut up. Until now he had always been polite and respectful, as well as generally cheerful. I wondered what had changed.

"You're fired. Get your own transportation home and send us the bill. I'll authorize a thousand a day plus expenses. You can wire the excess back from the deposit you got. Now you can speak if you have anything to say."

I was pale and trembling. I felt like a kid called to the principal's office. I managed to croak, "What about Gina?"

"We'll let the FBI and Canadian Police deal with the kidnapping. Due to your incompetence, we have spent a fortune and lost several days that could have been better employed. I'm just the yacht Captain, the lawyers will take charge now."

He stood up and stalked off without shaking hands. He did seem a bit pissed at me.

I was depressed. Had I really made things worse? It seemed that way. Focussing on the Persephone had drawn us far away from where Gina must have been taken, which would have to be Vancouver Island. By concentrating on the ship, we had ignored all other possibilities.

"Saga, what do we do now?" I put my head in my hands.

Saga answered sounding businesslike, "The first available commercial flight out of here is tomorrow morning on PenAir to Anchorage. Then Alaska Airlines, Anchorage to Seattle, Seattle to Vancouver. It will take about eleven hours including stops."

I was going to miss Gina's jet. "Okay. Book it."

I ordered a coffee and mulled over my position. I could just go back to Vancouver with my tail between my legs and admit failure. But I was seriously worried about Gina, and I didn't have confidence that the FBI and the Victoria police would even know where to start to find her now. The trail might be cold.

"Saga, change that booking to land in Victoria instead of Vancouver. I want to keep trying to find out what happened to Gina."

"Okay. I didn't want to distract you while you were busy playing pirate, but I have a lot of messages for you. Your mother called. Your ex-wife called. Detective Penrose called and emailed, Charlie called. Gina's lawyer called."

I had forgotten all about the rest of the world, I was so focussed on what Saga called "playing pirate". I began by reading Penrose's email.

*Dear Mr. Gray,*

*I haven't been able to reach you by phone. There have been several developments in the case of Gina's disappearance. On June 1, Peter Tombolo was found by a hunter. He was lost and wandering in the bush on Tzartus island. He was nearly delirious with hunger.*

*The RCMP from Port Alberni cleaned him up and took a statement. He claimed to have been kidnapped and his boat hijacked with him and Gina onboard. He claims the hijackers, two men, dumped him on a remote beach, but kept Gina and took off with the dinghy from Adonis. He called his company and they sent a car for him. The RCMP held him overnight, but in the absence of any evidence against him, they let him go on June 2. I believe he is back in San Francisco now.*

*Today, June 4, a fisherman found the dinghy from Adonis and reported it to the Coast Guard. It was drifting in Barkley sound near Bamfield. It was undamaged except for scratched bottom, probably from landing on a rocky beach. Forensics are going over it for prints.*

*Please call me as soon as you can.*

*Sincerely*

*Detective Carly Penrose*

*Victoria P.D.*

I glanced at the time on my phone. 11:49 AM. I called Charlie.

"Quant."

"Chan."

"I wondered if you were still alive. Have you rescued the damsel in distress?"

"Afraid not. I may have made her distress worse."

I spent about half an hour bringing him up to speed on events—making light of the plane crash—and told him I was heading back to Victoria. He promised to update Ollie and Feinman as soon as I hung up.

"One more thing. I'll be going into some rugged country. I'll need to rent a four-wheel drive SUV. Can you check around for me in Victoria to see what is available?"

"No need. My buddy Chumley lives in Uplands. He has a Land Rover he's lent me a few times. I'm sure he will do the same for you. He loves to help out."

Uplands was the old money area of Victoria. I imagined a Victorian pile with stables out the back, and a stiff-necked butler at the door.

"Thanks, Charlie, I appreciate that. Can you let him know I'm coming and email me his contact details?"

"Will do. Take care." He hung up.

I went back down to the restaurant for breakfast. I wasn't sleepy despite being up all night. Billy and the crew were there but I sat by myself at the opposite end of the room. I ordered coffee and an omelet. While I waited for my food I did an internal evaluation.

Billy was right. I had charged off after the obvious target without seriously considering the alternatives. The relationship between the names of the ship and the two boats seemed to tie it all together so neatly. And I was excited by the action-hero adventure of raiding a ship on the high seas. I must have thought I was in a Cussler novel.

How to find Gina? Time for real detective work. I wasn't a real detective, but I did have a lot of friends who were. Lisbeth Salander, Inspector Maigret, Poirot, Sam Spade, Marlowe, Miss Marple and yes, Sherlock Holmes. What would they do? Start with the evidence.

If I could find out where the dinghy landed, I could try to find witnesses who saw Gina with the two men. Barkley Sound was very lightly populated, with plenty of secluded beaches, but I was sure they would have landed near a road. There were a lot of logging roads in the area, in various states of disrepair. They must have had at least one other person to meet them with a vehicle, so we were probably looking for three men and a woman in an off-road capable vehicle.

I looked up as the waitress approached with my omelet. She was a sturdy Aleut woman of indeterminate age. She smiled, revealing a missing tooth, and set the plate down.

"Can I get you anything else?" I shook my head and she turned away. I was feeling non-verbal.

I ate in silence, but as I finished, I saw Vicky

coming over to my table. I motioned her to sit. She did. She wasn't smiling.

"Billy told us he fired you. It's none of my business, but I wanted to say I don't think you're such a bad guy. And Saga says she owes you her life, and I trust her. She and I plan to keep in touch. We'll be flying out to Cold Bay in an hour, so I may not see you again. Good Luck."

I stood up and mumbled goodbye, and put out my hand. She grabbed me in a brief bear hug, leaving me with bruised ribs but a slightly recovered ego.

David came over and told me the plane probably crashed because it was leaking after bashing the waves in rough seas. Bilge water flowing aft on takeoff would change the center of gravity, causing the bow to lift and stall. He said he was sorry I was fired.

One by one each of the crew members, except Billy, came over and expressed similar sentiments. Joe admitted that he had loved the raid, and said he hoped we could work together again sometime. There were handshakes but no more hugs. Soon they trooped out on their way back to Victoria.

I called Detective Penrose but got her voice mail. I left a message telling her the Persephone was clear, and that I'd be coming her way.

I talked to Saga. "There is only one main road from the Barkley Sound area, and it passes through Port Alberni. See if you can hack cameras in that area. We would be looking at May 29 and 30, four or more people, at least one of them a woman, leaving the area to head across the island. Try the ferry terminals too."

My reasoning was that all the major transportation

routes off Vancouver Island were on the east side. Ferries, airport, and marinas were all there. Anyone trying to escape the island would likely take a car ferry since that would not require ID. Commercial flights were out, but a private plane was a possibility. Of course, it was also possible that they were still on the island. I'd have to depend on Saga to find some evidence.

"Aye-Aye Captain. This may take a little while. It is a lot of data to sift through. At least sixty percent of the vehicles on that road are SUVs or pickups."

I paid the bill and went back up to my room. I still had another night before I could get back. When I saw the bed, fatigue caught up to me, and I undressed and climbed in. I fell into a deep sleep.

What seemed like seconds later, Saga said, "Time to wake up. My battery needs charging!"

Groggily I grumbled, "What time is it?"

"It is 8 PM. You have been asleep for almost seven hours."

I got up and went to pee. Then I plugged in the phone charger and got dressed. I left the camera glasses in the room with the phone and went down to get something to eat.

When I got to the lounge it was empty. The waitress, a blonde I guessed was close to my own age, brought me a Corona. On a sudden hunch, I asked her a question.

"Were you working last night?"

"Yeah, I was here until closing."

"Were there any Japanese people in here last

night?"

"Oh, you mean the crew of the Persephone. Yeah, about fifteen of them were here last night. They chopper over every few weeks when the ship is passing nearby. They sing Karaoke, eat burgers and drink beer, except for the pilot. Then they leave."

"Did they behave differently last night?"

"Nah, same as usual."

"Were there any women with them?"

"Just the cook, who I think is female, although she's bigger than most of the men."

I ordered another Corona and a cheeseburger. It seemed the Persephone was probably unconnected with Gina's abduction. I wondered what the crew thought when they got back and discovered the loading door open. I chuckled to myself. I was glad we didn't do any other damage since they were most likely completely innocent. Anyway, we gave them a mystery to talk about on the long trip to Tokyo.

I marshaled my thoughts. So, Gina was taken ashore and then transported somewhere else by car. Or boat. Despite homeland security, it was absurdly easy to enter US waters from Canada in a small boat without clearing customs. But maybe the kidnappers were Canadian? The Japanese connection now sounded like a dead end. So many possibilities. We would have to follow an evidence trail of some sort, but the time I had wasted chasing the Persephone had allowed the trail to grow cold.

I finished my burger, drank another Corona, and went back to my room. I tuned the TV to CNN. There was a report of a Japanese RO-RO which capsized off the Aleutians. Video showed it awash on its side. Apparently, the stern door failed and big seas flooded the car deck. The crew escaped in a helicopter they had on deck. The Coast Guard was investigating. I felt guilty for a moment, but then I remembered the crew had been partying when they should have been on board. Tough luck for them. I went back to the job at hand.

"Saga, any luck finding the SUV?"

"Nada. There are surveillance cameras at the three filling stations on the road through town, but nowhere else. There were quite a few vehicles with four people, usually two men and two women. Nobody looked like Gina, and none of the women seemed to be a prisoner or drugged. If they didn't need fuel, we would miss them."

"Okay. Maybe they thought of the cameras. Try looking for a single person in an SUV or four-door pickup heading West on Saturday, Sunday or Monday at the latest. It is likely they would buy fuel on the way in at least."

"Okay, give me a few minutes."

While she was searching, I dug out my laptop computer, set it up on the desk and connected to the net. Then I Googled "Gina Lee Disappearance".

There were a lot of results, but one caught my eye. It was a CNN video on YouTube. Anderson Cooper was interviewing Peter Tombolo. His story was pretty much as Penrose said, but a few things were interesting.

"How did they lure Gina onboard the Adonis?" Cooper asked.

"I did that. They held me at gunpoint. All I did was invite her on board for a coffee. She glanced at her watch, shrugged and said she had time. I'd hoped she would say no. As soon as we were below they grabbed her and tied her up."

"Did you see their faces?"

"Yes, but not the greatest look, as they both wore hoodies and sunglasses. I gave a full description to the police." Tombolo didn't look too stressed and had obviously recovered well from his wilderness ordeal.

The camera cut from Tombolo to a picture of Gina in a business suit. Anyone who saw her was requested to contact the FBI. Then they moved on to the antics of the idiots and thieves running for President.

I would have to talk to Tombolo.

Saga said, "Eleven AWD vehicles with room for four people and a single driver stopped for fuel in the target period. I ran the plates on all of them to see if anything seemed familiar. All but two had BC plates. Those had Washington state tags. I eliminated three of the BC cars as they were also seen leaving Port Alberni later, with no additional passengers."

"Was any of the ones left a rental?"

"Yes, there was a Jeep Cherokee, driven by a woman, with BC plates, registered to EZ Rentals in Nanaimo."

"See if you can spot that car in any other camera on Vancouver Island, anytime since Monday."

"Oui Mon Cherie. Give me some time."

I sat down with a pad and pen provided by the

hotel. Despite my comfort with electronic communication, sometimes writing things down helps me to get a grip. I started to make a list of key characters in the case and what I knew about them or thought I knew.

Gina Lee – wealthy real estate investor, world traveler. I knew very little about Gina. My personal connection to her was based on just two meetings.

Peter Tombolo – businessman, investor. Gina's half brother. Again, I knew very little beyond that.

Genyosha? We now had zero reasons to suspect the Japanese. I crossed this one out.

Detective Carly Penrose – in charge of abduction case.

Tracy Wagner – Gina's personal assistant. Worth talking to?

Billy Taylor – Boat captain. I put him on the list mainly because of his sudden change of attitude towards my involvement. I couldn't help thinking something else was going on.

The ransom demand. Maybe we better go back to that?

Saga interrupted my musings.

"I have something. That rental car filled up with fuel in Comox on Wednesday, June 1 at about 3 PM. The photo shows four people in it. Faces not clear but it looks like a man driving with a woman in the passenger seat. Rear passengers indistinct."

"Thank you, Saga. Keep the photo. We'll need to ask questions at motels and hotels along the path. There aren't a huge number, thank goodness. From

Comox, there is a Ferry to Powell River. See if they took that. Also, see if the car rental company will tell you anything. Too late tonight I suppose. What time is our flight tomorrow?"

"12:40 PM. It was the earliest they have."

"I guess I'll have to live with that. Can you find out if a printer is available in the hotel? I'd like you to print out anything new you have on Peter Tombolo. Better do Gina too."

"Whatever." She sounded like a sulky teenager. I didn't take it personally, I figured she was just trying on voices the way some women try on clothes.

It was late. I had a shower, brushed my teeth and turned in. No need to wake up too early the next day, so no alarm.

# 21 THE HOLLOW CHOCOLATE BUNNIES OF THE APOCALYPSE

*I was in a windowless cellar, chained to the floor, my head on a rough stone block. Flickering yellow light came from above, like candles. I heard a scraping sound, and a large ax blade was dragged across the floor in front of me. It was filthy with what looked like dried blood. Behind the ax came a large pair of feet in heavy leather sandals. I was puzzled. Shouldn't the feet have come first?*

*I heard a loud grunt, and the sound of something swishing through the air, followed by a thump. A round object rolled across my view. It was a yellow melon with a blue smiley face painted on it.*

"Your Mother is Calling." The phone was saying, repeatedly. I swam to the surface of consciousness and answered.

"Gray."

"Chan, where are you. You haven't been answering my calls."

"Dutch Harbor. It's in the Aleutians."

"I know very well where it is. I went there on my Alaska cruise a few years ago." Most people take Alaska Cruises in a luxury cruise liner. My mother and her sister spent a month there a few years ago using BC and Alaska ferries, buses, trains, and for all I know, dog sleds. They don't observe the normal constraints of tourism.

"Can I call you when I get home? I have a plane to catch." That was completely true, but I had no idea what time it was.

"See that you do." She hung up.

The message light was blinking on the hotel phone. I picked it up and read the instructions for checking messages. After pressing several digits, I got a robotic voice.

"Your printing is ready for pickup at the front desk."

"Thanks," I said to the dial tone. "Saga, what time is it?"

"8:42 AM. You slept a long time."

It was Sunday morning. Business calls would have to wait. I showered, dressed and went downstairs. On my way to the restaurant, I picked up what Saga had printed. It was the size of something by Tolstoy. Sometimes too much information can be worse than too little.

Over my eggs and bacon, I skimmed the dossiers of Tombolo and Lee. A few things caught my eye and I circled them. Tombolo owned a computer security firm called SEKURTAB which offered its services to corporations and governments. He had several other companies in unrelated fields. Gina's realty company was publicly traded on the NASDAQ exchange as GLHS. It had gross revenues of more than a billion a year. She was on the boards of several charities.

There were a few news stories in which they were both mentioned, mostly society pages. Gina's biography indicated she was an adopted boat person, but the word "orphan" never appeared. This made me wonder if she had at least one living parent.

By the time I finished my ninth cup of coffee, it was time to pack up and get to the airport. They wanted you there two hours before flight time, thanks to Homeland Security, no matter how unlikely a terrorist threat was in the Aleutians.

It was a long boring trip back to Victoria. I couldn't even talk to Saga as there was no internet most of the time. However, her server was continuing its work while we were in the air. I continued to read what she had on Gina. It was repetitive, but the theme was clear. Gina was successful, generous, and kind to stray puppies. But I was sure that you don't get that rich without stepping on a few toes. I wondered who her enemies were? It would have to wait.

We arrived late at night. A room at the Empress had been booked. I was returning to the scene of the crime so to speak. An airport limo got us there through the light evening traffic. I checked in and went straight to bed.

In the morning Saga had coffee sent up. I started making phone calls, Detective Penrose first.

"Penrose."

"Chandler Gray. I got your email. Thanks for keeping me in the loop. Are there any further developments?"

"Hi Chan. My email had just about everything in it. Tombolo is trying to get Adonis back. Are you filing a claim for salvage?"

"I suppose I should. I promised the crew of Aphrodite a share of whatever we get."

"If you can deal directly with him you might be

able to avoid the courts. Cases like that can take years."

"Good idea. Can you let me have his contact details?"

"I'll email them to you. Are you back in town?"

"Yes, I'm at the Empress now, but I'm planning to check out today. Can you give me contact info for Gina's P.A, Tracy Wagner?"

"She's still at the Empress in the same suite. I got the impression she's a bit lost without Gina to give her orders. Ask for Gina when you call, the room is still in her name."

"One more thing. Do you know the color of the bottom paint on Adonis' dinghy?"

"Yes, it was a light pastel blue."

I thanked her and promised to keep in touch, then hung up. Then I called the hotel operator and asked to be connected to Gina Lee's room.

"Gina Lee's room."

"Is that Tracy? This is Chandler Gray."

"Yes, Mr. Gray. I remember you. Thank you for rescuing me from that thug."

"I'm in the hotel. Could we meet in the Q for breakfast? I want to talk with you about Gina.

"Yes, I would like that. Would twenty minutes be alright?"

I put on a blazer, unplugged the phone from the charger and pocketed it. I asked Saga if there were any new developments but there was nothing of import.

She wasn't sarcastic or rude. That concerned me a bit.

Tracy was already there when I walked into the dining room. I almost didn't recognize her, except she was the only blonde sitting alone. The pink streak was gone from her hair, which was professionally styled in wavy tendrils. She was wearing a green knit dress which set off her athletic figure perfectly. As I approached she stood up and surprised me with a warm hug. I noticed her eyes were green too.

"Hello, Mr. Gray."

"Please call me Chan. People who call me Mr. Gray are usually bill collectors. You look incredible, Tracy"

"Okay, Chan. You can call me Tracy." I had already done that.

We made a bit of small talk and then I asked what she had been doing since Gina disappeared.

"Mostly answering phone calls. I had Gina's cell calls routed to my phone, and I have been dealing with her friends and associates, mostly calling to ask if I know anything new. I don't. When I'm with Gina I'm always very busy, but now I had time to go to the spa and buy some new clothes." That explained her transformed appearance. Of course, the last time I saw her she had been abducted and brutalized.

"I suppose you know I spent the night with Gina before she disappeared."

Tracy blushed and looked down. "Yes. She said you were...capable."

My face colored too. "I was under the impression

you didn't see her that morning."

"I didn't. She sent me a text before she left for the boat. You were still sleeping."

I told her about my plan to try and trace Gina's movements by finding the landing site. She surprised me with a request.

"Can I come with you? I'm going stir crazy here, and I'd really like to try to help rescue Gina."

I couldn't think of a good reason to say no, and frankly, I found her company pleasant. I called Charlie's friend Chumley, whose name turned out to be spelled Cholmondeley, and he told me the car was ready for me. I told Tracy I'd pick up the car and come back to fetch her. That would give her time to change into casual clothes and pack a bag.

It was only a ten-minute cab ride to the Cholmondeley mansion. It wasn't a Victorian house, as I had imagined, but a stone empire style mansion with a circular driveway and a large porte-cochère.

The modern Land Rover LR4 I had planned to rent was a splendid machine with a powerful V8 engine, air conditioning, navigation, and all the other amenities one would expect. The machine parked in the driveway bore no resemblance to that. It was straight out of an old Safari movie. The olive drab Landie had to be at least fifty years old but looked to be in decent shape. I walked around it. There was a spare tire strapped to the hood—bonnet I mean—and two more on the back. There were winches on both ends. I looked in the window and could see that it had three gearshift levers.

I walked up and knocked on the door using a large

ring gripped in the jaws of a bronze lion. The sound of doors opening and closing was followed by hollow footsteps. The door creaked open. The gentleman standing there had to be at least ninety but looked much older. His face had as many lines as a roadmap of Britain. His watery blue eyes and large red beak topped a regimental mustache with waxed ends. His back was ramrod straight, and he offered me his hand.

"Chandler Gray." I tried to sound military.

"Major Eustace Chumley. Old Sam Gray's boy, eh?"

My father's name was Keith, but I didn't argue.

"I'm here about the Land Rover."

"Oh yes. Brought her back from Inja. Splendid machine. The Maharaja and I…"

He launched into a long story about tiger hunting, the British Raj, and extra-hot curry. I heard footsteps on the gravel drive behind me and turned to see a man about my own age, wiping his hands on a rag. The Major continued droning on in the background.

"Chumley. I see you've met the Major." He made a circle around his ear. "He's a few cartridges short of a full load. You must be Chan. Charlie says you're a good guy, and I always believe Charlie."

We shook hands. He led me over to the antique Land Rover and gave me the keys. I got in on the left side. The steering wheel was on the right. I moved over awkwardly and started it up. He showed me how to operate the levers for the transfer case and the low range. "If you manage to get her stuck, use the winches. Either one can lift the whole weight of the thing."

"I'll return it in a few days. Thanks so much for this."

The engine sounded like a farm tractor. As I pulled it around out of the driveway I realized it had been a very long time since I drove a vehicle without power steering and brakes. There is only one word to describe the ride. Rough. And one for the performance. Slow.

Back at the Empress I collected my gear and checked out. Tracy was waiting in the lobby. When she saw the Land Rover, she smiled.

"Cool car! This should be fun."

She got in on the wrong side. After that was straightened out we headed north.

# 22 THE DOUBLE COMFORT SAFARI CLUB

As we headed up to Port Alberni, Tracy and I got to know each other. She was a cheerful and amusing companion. The Landie couldn't do more than 50 miles per hour—the old speedo read in miles—so we had to pull over occasionally to let faster traffic go by.

I took a detour to Cowichan Bay so we could have lunch at Hilary's Cheese. My friends there treated us royally. I declined the wine pairing but Tracy took a glass.

I gave Tracy a brief biography, then told her in detail about the Persephone adventure, as I was now calling it. She was particularly interested in Saga's role. All through our conversation, the phone was silent, but I knew Saga was listening.

Shortly after noon, we were in Port Alberni, and we stopped at Boomerangs Café for a coffee. I had found a topographical map of the area in the Land Rover, and we went over it while we ate.

The logging road that went closest to the place where we found Adonis ran on Vancouver Island behind the Alma Russel Islands. It came near the beach in several places but didn't go right down, at least on the map.

"Saga, can you get me the latest satellite photos of the beach in Julia Passage behind the Alma Russel Islands?"

"What's the magic word?" She used her severe British voice.

# TIGER AND THE ROBOT

"Uhh...Please?" My Gran used to do that to me. I felt like a kid, but not in a good way.

The photos showed three places where there appeared to be a trail down to the beach, not shown on the map. Saga offered an opinion.

"I don't think that is the right area. Even though it is a little closer to the place we found Adonis, it is on the North side of Alberni inlet, and the roads there are very convoluted. Anyway, we should go from where they found Tombolo, which was the south side of Tzartus Island."

Tracy looked at the map, "Saga's right. I think we should look there first."

I was outnumbered. After I paid the bill and tipped the cute Aussie waitress, we got in the car and headed south down Franklin River road. It was a paved two-lane road in good shape. It did make sense that the kidnappers would want to stay on the pavement if possible.

The road wound through second growth forest with the odd cabin off to one side or the other. We continued into Bamfield Road which was gravel and a bit rougher, but still not bad. Then we bore right onto an unnamed track which would hit the beach opposite Tzartus Island. It was very rough and bumpy, but still no real challenge for the Land Rover.

When we got to the beach we got out and walked. Tracy had brought hiking boots, I just had my topsiders. "What are we looking for?"

"The dinghy that they found had scratches on the bottom. It had light blue bottom paint and I figure it would have left marks on the beach."

"And what if we find blue paint on the rocks? What then? Is blue paint rare?"

"We ask the locals if they saw anything."

"What locals? Look around. There is nobody here."

She was right. There were a couple of float houses visible out in the Sound, but we couldn't get to them without a boat. We walked the beach some but didn't find anything.

Tracy said, "You need to find somebody who saw Gina. We have no idea who she was with so we have to look for Gina. I brought some photos with me."

"Saga has photos of her too. If we take that tack then the logical place to start is Port Alberni, since all the traffic from this area goes through there and it has restaurants, bars and filling stations."

"If you wanted to get someone out of here against their will, and take a ferry, what would be the best vehicle for the job?"

I slapped myself on the forehead. I had been thinking of an SUV, but a motorhome or trailer would make more sense. With a head and galley onboard and curtains on the windows, it would be easy to keep someone hidden.

"A motorhome?"

"Bingo. If they used one of those, chances are nobody saw Gina at all." Tracy was a better detective than me.

"Listen to Tracy, Bozo. She makes sense." Saga said. "I'll check the surveillance cameras for motorhomes. I didn't see too many on the way out here."

I turned the Land Rover around and we started back towards Port Alberni. About five miles up the road a big black pickup came up behind us fast, horn blaring and lights flashing, kicking up dust and gravel behind it. We were still in the rough single track part, and there wasn't much room to pull over, but I put two wheels in the brush to make room for them. The trucked gunned by us then slewed to a stop diagonally across the road. I hit the brakes hard and stopped a few feet short of a collision.

The doors of the pickup opened. The passenger got out right in front of me. He was a young guy in a camo outfit, about my height—just over six feet—but a lot heavier. The driver came around the front of the truck, and he was even bigger. They didn't look armed, and we definitely weren't.

They came up on each side of the cab, the bigger guy on Tracy's side. I dropped the gearshift in reverse, just in case. He knocked on her window. Windows on those old Landies don't roll down, they slide back half way. Tracy slid the window open a crack with her left hand while reaching into her purse with her right. I wondered if she had a gun in there. She was American after all...

"Can I help you?" Tracy asked, sounding like the clerk in a store.

The jerk pushed the window as far open as it would go, and reached out to touch Tracy's cheek.

"Ain't this a pretty thing." His words were slurred with alcohol. On my side, the other thug was reaching for the door handle. I heard a scream to my left. I unlatched my door and kicked it hard. The corner caught the guy right in the middle of his face, and he fell back, bleeding from the nose. I glanced to my left. The other thug was writhing on the ground, rubbing his eyes.

"Bear spray." Tracy grinned.

I slammed the door, floored the throttle and reversed down the road as fast as the old car would go, which was not very. Then I spun the wheel and hit the brakes, backing off the road. I crunched the transfer lever into four-wheel drive and trundled off toward the water. Behind us the big pickup was backing and filling, trying to turn around on the narrow road.

For the first few hundred yards a kid on a bicycle could have outrun us but eventually, we got moving as fast as the tiny winding track would allow.

"Saga, call 911."

"No service."

"We had cell service on the beach earlier. Try again when you get a signal."

I heard the roar of a big V8 behind us. The pickup was gaining on us, but not a lot. He knew the road ended at the beach, so he wasn't in a hurry.

"911, for what place please." The phone came to life.

"Bamfield."

I explained about the assault and that we were being followed. The operator connected us to the Port Alberni RCMP post.

"Constable McEwen." A woman's voice.

"We are on the unnamed road which dead ends at the beach south of Tzartus Island. Two louts tried to assault us, but we turned around and escaped. They are following us in a pickup."

I gave her the license number.

She chuckled. "Daryl and Kyle Lewis. I know them. I'll phone Daryl and put the fear of God in him. When you get to the end of the road, turn left along the beach. What sort of vehicle do you have?"

"Land Rover." I didn't say it was an antique.

"That should be fine. Pick your way along the beach until you come to a house. Pull in alongside and wait. The Lewis boys won't go there."

"Why not?"

"They know it's my mother's house. And they know she's handy with a shotgun."

She hung up. The truck was close behind us now. Suddenly its engine roared and the big bumper appeared to fill my rearview mirror. With a BANG we lurched forward as he rammed us. Then he backed off. I could see the passenger answering a cell phone.

Around the next corner, I could see the beach. I braked and dropped into second gear and swung left as fast as I could. The beach was made of smooth round stones, and we slid around a bit. Tracy looked back.

"They are still coming."

I zig and zagged avoiding boulders I judged big enough to do damage. Behind us, the pickup fell back. It just wasn't as nimble as the Rover. After a few hundred yards a house came into view. It was up a steep bank from the beach. I stopped at the bottom and put the Rover in low range. Then gunned it forward. It moved at a snail's pace in first gear. I shifted into second where it moved at tortoise speed. But it climbed the sandy, near vertical bank without hesitation and soon we rolled up beside the house next to an old Toyota Land Cruiser. The phone rang. My heart was beating so hard it almost drowned out the ring.

"Gray."

"Mom's expecting you. Just knock on the door and introduce yourselves."

"Thanks so much. This is beyond the call."

"No worries. Are those jerks still behind you?"

"Yes, but they are on the beach trying to turn around."

"Want to press charges?"

"We have it all on video, which I'll send you. I suggest you just keep it in reserve and give them a severe warning." We said our goodbyes and hung up.

Tracy laughed. "Where I come from in Montana, the cops would pick them up and beat the crap out of them, then dump them off in the woods somewhere."

We climbed out of the car and went to the door of the house, which was really just a cabin. The door opened before we got there. The woman who opened it was South Asian, with long black hair, wearing jeans and a plaid logger's shirt. Her big black eyes sparkled and she smiled, revealing even white teeth.

I must have looked confused.

"My daughter Simi said you'd be coming. I'm Amrita Grewal. McEwen was my husband's name."

"Chandler Gray. This is Tracy Wagner."

Amrita was probably no more than fifty, and very attractive. Not pretty in a conventional way, her animated smile and darkly reflective eyes gave her a friendly air. She led us into the combined kitchen and dining room, where a pot of tea was steeping. On the wall, there were photos of her in various glamorous poses, some with other good-looking people I didn't recognize. No wedding pictures. I imagined she was a retired Bollywood star, but I didn't comment.

Tracy and Amrita were soon fast friends, talking about their families and pets. I only half listened. I had Saga email about five minutes of video to Constable McEwen. Then I went over and looked out the window. The pickup was gone.

It was almost dinner time. I thought we should get back to Port Alberni. We took our leave of Amrita after she exchanged email addresses with Tracy and promised to stay in touch. She told us how to get to the main road from her longish driveway.

It was a two-hour drive back to Port Alberni. On the way, Saga booked us two adjoining rooms in the Riverside Motel. I was still on edge after what happened but there were no further incidents. We checked into our rooms and agreed to go for dinner after thirty minutes to freshen up. I had a badly needed shower and put on a clean shirt.

When I knocked on Tracy's door she stepped out in a form-fitting black dress with spaghetti straps. I mentally upgraded the dinner destination from a diner to a real restaurant. Saga guided us to the Starboard

Grill where we sat on the Terrace overlooking the lake. We shared a bottle of Pinot Grigio and ate fresh local salmon. The food was nothing fancy but the company was great.

Tracy acted as if we were on a date, touching my arm every so often, and speaking softly.

"I was impressed by how you handled that confrontation." She chuckled.

"It was you that subdued that brute with Bear Spray. He didn't know what hit him!"

Saga interrupted our laughter. "I found the getaway vehicle."

Tracy said, "Was it a motorhome?"

"Not exactly. I looked at about a dozen motorhomes. All of them had kids, or dogs, or both. Then I looked at commercial vans and trucks. One caught my attention. It was a five-ton truck, white with a box on the back. A sign on the door said Stevenson Plumbing and a toll-free number. I called the number but it belonged to another company. Then I checked the license plates, which were from Oregon. They belong to a Subaru sedan from Portland, so most likely stolen. It was in the ferry lineup from Comox heading to Powell River on Wednesday morning."

"Better let Detective Penrose know about that vehicle. It has a five-day start on us, so I'm not sure if it is worth following it. See if you can find it in any other ferry lineup. The only way it could leave the Sunshine Coast is by ferry, either Egmont or back the way it came. Or Texada Island, which seems unlikely. Look for a similar vehicle with different plates and/or signage."

With the business taken care of, I paid the bill and took Tracy's arm. We drove back to the motel. I opened the car door for her and walked with her to her room. At the door, she turned her face up to me for a kiss. I kissed her gently on the lips, not too long, then stepped back.

"Shall I wake you in the morning? We should get an early start."

She grabbed my wrist and pulled me into her room.

# 23 THE GODS OF NEWPORT

Newport Harbor High School was a public school, but Tiggy's fellow students almost all came from rich families, many of them famous. The top students were almost all white. Tiggy was the exception. She was clever, but even more important, highly motivated. Every time one of those blonde-haired blue-eyed cheerleader types call her "Chink" or "Gook" she just smiled and won another award.

She participated in sailing and swimming at school and excelled at both, particularly sailing. As the only minority on the team, her skill, determination, and pure will-to-win gained the respect, if not the friendship of the other sailors.

Excellent nutrition and health care had helped her to grow taller than the average Asian, and sports gave her a toned physique. In her Senior year, she began to insist on being called Gina, not Tiggy. Contact lenses replaced her round wire-rims and she discovered makeup. Her casual clothes were upgraded to modest, but elegant dresses. The boys noticed her for the first time, one in particular.

His nickname was Bully, short for Bulldozer. He was Captain of the Football team, known as the Sailors, and was on the sailing team too. Bully was tall, blonde and muscular. He wore his hair in a military crew cut, which made his thick neck look even thicker. Despite his name, Gina had not seen him bully anyone.

He seemed to have his pick of girls. When he met a pretty one in the hall, he'd smile, and she'd look up at him adoringly, hanging on his every word. Except for Gina, who ignored him completely. She was focused on who she was going to be, and her plans didn't include falling for a football idol. Besides, she could outsail him anytime, and his marks were not anywhere close to hers.

Near the end of the school year, the Senior Prom took place. Gina didn't plan to attend. One day, Bully approached her in the hallway.

"Do you have a date for the prom?" He asked.

"That's none of your business." Gina unconsciously shook her head.

Bully looked down at her. "Sorry. I said that wrong. Would you be my date for the prom?"

Gina looked up. His face had a desperate pleading look, his blue eyes seemed close to tears. She felt a pang of sympathy for the big lug.

"I'll give it some consideration and let you know." She said, and turned on her heel to go to class.

The next morning when she left for school, Bully was standing outside the door of her home on the Lido Peninsula, holding a bouquet of flowers. She took them from him. Nobody had ever brought her flowers before. She smiled and thanked him, then took the flowers inside and gave them to her Mother, who winked knowingly.

Bully rode the bus to school with her, although he had a car. A 450SL Mercedes, popular with rich kids in Newport Beach.

On the night of the Prom, a white stretch limo arrived to pick up Gina. Bully, in a black tuxedo, handed her an orchid corsage and opened the door for her.

The Prom was packed, but Gina stood out like a rose in a field of violets. Her dress was the simplest one there, a formal red Cheongsam with a slit on one side. She wore her hair straight and unadorned. The other girls whispered to each other when she came in arm-in-arm with Bully. Most of them were jealous.

The evening started off well. Bully wasn't a bad dancer for a big guy. Whenever another boy asked her to dance, Bully stared him off. This annoyed Gina.

"You don't own me, just because I came to the Prom with you."

"Sorry."

It didn't matter. No more boys asked her. At the end of the evening, Ashley Davis was crowned Prom Queen. Bully was crowned Prom King. Afterward he danced with Ashley, a tall blonde with movie star looks. Gina thought Ashley was a bimbo, but she wasn't jealous. She didn't really like Bully that much.

After one dance with Ashley, Billy came back to her. He suggested they leave and go to an after-party, where they could get a drink. The Prom was alcohol-free.

"No. Take me home."

Bully shrugged. As soon as they were in the limo, he slid over beside her and put his arm around her. He kissed her gently on the lips and she didn't resist. It was her first kiss--except. Memories of the sailing instructor giving her mouth-to-mouth filled her mind.

Then Bully forced his tongue into her mouth and

slid his hand up under her dress. She turned into Tiger and fought him off. The car stopped at a red light. Gina threw the door open and lunged out. She caught a glimpse of Bully's bright red, angry face just before the door slammed and the car drove off.

Gina never spoke to him again. He started hanging out with Ashley.

After graduation, she told Edith she wanted to go to college as far away as possible. With her marks and SAT scores, she could have her choice of schools. Stanford wasn't all that far away geographically, but culturally it was worlds from Newport Beach. She enrolled in Economics.

## 24 FOLLOW THE MONEY

I woke up feeling guilty. I didn't feel guilty because I slept with Tracy. I felt guilty because I enjoyed it. I felt disloyal to Gina, even though I had never promised her anything. She never promised me anything either. There wasn't time before she was taken.

Tracy was up, making coffee in the kitchenette. She was wearing a longish t-shirt, nothing else. Somehow she managed to look innocent and sexy at the same time. She brought me a coffee and sat on the bed beside me. She tousled my hair and kissed me for a long time. I reached up under the t-shirt…

Later she rolled on her back and said, "Last night was wonderful, my best experience ever. This morning too. Gina was right. You are capable."

"It was great for me too," I said with a grin. Tracy wasn't as seductive as Gina, but she was passionate and eager and knew her way around a man's body. If Gina wasn't occupying a metaphorical space in the bed, Tracy and I could be falling in love.

As if reading my thoughts, Tracy said, "There is something you should know about Gina. She isn't into long term relationships."

Before I could answer the phone said, "Your Mother is calling."

I picked up. "Chan here."

"Are you busy?"

"At the moment I'm in bed with a beautiful

blonde in Port Alberni. We are on a quest to rescue a kidnapped billionaire. Other than that, I don't have much going on."

"In that case, could you come over and fix my computer? I'm having trouble accessing the internet."

"Seriously? Call Brophy. I really am in Port Alberni. Gotta go."

I hung up.

I went to my own room, showered, packed up and checked us out. I took Tracy's bag to the Land Rover. I noticed it had a few fresh marks from the previous day's adventure. We stopped at the Steampunk Café for a coffee and muffin. We talked about our next move. First Saga updated us on the truck.

"No sign of the truck on any other ferry. It must still be on the Sunshine Coast. That doesn't mean Gina is there, they could have left by boat or plane, or a different vehicle. A similar truck was reported stolen in Saanich about ten days ago, so that is probably where it came from."

Tracy said, "I can't see how we are going to find her this way. Saga, do you have any ideas for finding Gina?"

"I thought you'd never ask. Yes. I think we should follow the money."

"What money? As far as I know money hasn't come into it." I might have sounded a bit annoyed.

"Don't be shirty. What about the ransom? I say we pay it and see who collects."

"How will we pay two billion? Even Gina's lawyers can't raise that much, and they were given instructions not to pay."

"I can do it. There are two inactive numbered accounts in a Cayman Islands bank which total 2.3 billion US. They belonged to two Colombian traficantes, both killed by competitors. I have hacked the passwords. I can pay the ransom from those accounts and trace the routing. Later I'll reverse the transactions."

"I'm impressed. Maybe you should just take over, and give me a call when Gina is released." I wasn't trying to be sarcastic, really.

"Thanks. But I might still need you for transportation. Maybe they will release her if they believe the ransom has been paid."

Tracy said, "We should ask for proof that she is alive, then try to negotiate the ransom down. Nobody pays the asking price. Don't you watch TV?"

"No." Saga and I answered simultaneously.

"Good idea, Tracy. I'll call the lawyer and see if there have been more ransom demands."

"Saga, can you call Jonathan Roberts? Wait. Not too private here. Let's get in the car first." I noticed some people at the next table looking at us. They might have heard two billion dollars mentioned...

One thing great about the BC coast. You can get a brilliantly sunny day any time of the year. The converse is also true. You can get a miserable, cold, wet day any time of year. While we were in the coffee shop, a mist had descended and turned to a heavy rain.

We ran to the car. I started it up and turned on the

wipers. They were slow and feeble. The windows misted over in seconds. After some messing with the heater controls I got the defroster going, which cleared a small patch at the bottom of the windshield. I wiped the inside of the window with my sleeve and drove off. The Land Rover was by no means watertight. Water came in at the base of the windshield, through the side windows and under the doors. It reminded me of Ollie's boat Disturbance in the Vic-Maui race.

Once moving, Saga got Roberts on the line. I let Tracy talk to him as she knew him quite well. The phone was on speaker so we could all hear.

"Jonathan Roberts."

"Hi, Jon. This is Tracy Walters. Do you remember me?"

"Of course, how could I forget?" He sounded warmer than the last time we spoke.

"I'm here with Chandler Gray. We want to discuss ransom for Gina."

His voice went cold. "I understood Mr. Gray had been fired."

"Billy fired him. I have re-hired him. He has an imaginative way to pay the ransom. It won't cost Gina anything. Have you had any more ransom demands?"

"Several. The last one came in just a short while ago. Not answering was a good negotiating tactic, the ask is now 800 million."

"It still isn't pocket change. How do you get in touch with them?"

"Each demand has a new email address. They say

we need to respond within thirty minutes or the address will be offline."

"Is it too late to answer the last one?"

"Maybe five minutes to go."

"Okay, please email them and say we are considering paying the ransom, but need proof Gina is alive."

"Will do. Can I call you back on this number?"

"Yes. It's Chan's cell phone. I'll talk to you." She hung up.

I voiced some concern. "How will we get Gina back alive? Her captors might kill her as soon as they have the money, or believe they have it."

Saga said, "We should negotiate a public place for them to release her, and I won't transfer the money until we can see her. I will send them a small deposit, say ten million, to let them know we are serious, and to test the transfer."

"If they tell us where they will release her, it will give us a strong hint as to where they are holding her. It seems to me it would be best to take the offensive and snatch her from them before the handoff."

Tracy said, "We have no idea where she is. She could be almost anywhere in the world right now, although I'm inclined to think she's in BC or Washington State. They could do what they did with Tombolo and dump her in the woods somewhere."

Trying to think like a kidnapper, I said, "If I were doing something like this, I'd tie her up somewhere secluded, and get well away before saying where she was. I would insist on full payment before giving the coordinates."

Tracy was still worried. "That makes sense, but they might think of some other way. Anyway, transferring small amounts is easy, but 800 million is way too much for the gray market, only the biggest banks could handle it."

"Don't worry about that part, I have worked out how to do it. Details will have to wait until we get banking info."

The phone played the theme from Jaws. My ex-wife's ringtone. I sent it to voicemail.

We were almost in Nanaimo, and the rain had let up when the phone rang again the regular ringtone. California area code. It was Roberts. Tracy picked up.

"Hi Jon, what do you have for us."

"I just got an email back, from a different address. They promised to send a photo with today's news headlines. I'll forward it to your number as soon as I get it."

After she hung up we had a decision to make.

"I really should return the Land Rover to Chumley, but I also want to get back to Vancouver as soon as possible. We'll probably have to travel somewhere to get Gina, but we have no idea where. Vancouver has the best options."

"Let's leave the Land Rover near the BC Ferry terminal, and go as foot passengers. We can have a towing company pick it up and deliver it to Chumley on a flatbed."

Tracy always seemed to have a practical solution. We left it at a gas station near Departure Bay. I gave the boss two hundred dollars and the key. He arranged the towing to Chumley's.

We hoofed it to the terminal and bought tickets. While we were waiting, I called Chumley. I thanked him and asked him to bill me for the damage to the Land Rover. I gave him the phone number of the garage arranging the tow.

"What sort of damage?"

"A few scratches from driving through the underbrush. Maybe a dent on the back bumper."

"Bah, we call that patina. Adds to the authenticity. I won't be sending a bill unless it's a basket case."

I thanked him again and hung up. Charlie certainly had some great friends. We soon got on the ferry and traipsed up to the dining room for a late lunch. As we cleared Newcastle Island, the ferry began a long slow roll. It was blowing hard from the Northwest, at least 30 knots judging by the whitecaps. Tracy was eating her White Spot pasta with gusto.

"I was under the impression that you suffered from seasickness. You look fine to me."

She blushed. "What gave you that idea?"

"Billy told me that was why you didn't go on the Swiftsure Race."

"I might have told him I got seasick as a tactful way of avoiding going along. The truth is I just don't like sailing on big fancy boats like Aphrodite. But I don't get sick."

"That's good. We'll be sleeping on my boat tonight unless you prefer a hotel."

"Is it a big fancy boat?"

"Well, it would have been considered such fifty years ago. Now it is on the dinky side. Forty feet. An old Hinckley."

She nodded, "Okay, I hope it has a double berth."

"Kind of vee-shaped and tight, but yes."

I thought about which of my friends could be pressed into picking us up at the Horseshoe Bay ferry terminal. Feinman had a white minivan he called Moby. The trouble was, the seats were always out so he could carry assorted musical instruments and electronic devices to festivals and other venues. Ollie's Alfa had only two seats. That left Charlie.

I called Charlie Quant and told him about our adventures in the Land Rover. I also asked if he could pick us up at the ferry. He agreed but said it would be nice to have more notice next time. Before he hung up he said, "Are you sure that attack was random? You would have been easy to spot in that car. Maybe you were being warned off?"

"It didn't occur to me but I'll call the RCMP constable and suggest it. Thanks!"

After he hung up I called Constable McEwen on her direct number, which she had kindly given me.

"McEwen."

"Chandler Gray."

"Oh Hi. I was thinking of calling you. What's up?"

"Do you think there is a possibility the Lewis boys were paid to attack us? My friend Charlie said it sounded planned to him."

"It is possible. They advertise as handymen on Craigslist. I'll find out and get back to you."

"Thanks. You should be able to reach me on this number."

I looked up at Tracy. She was finished her lunch and looking out the window at the view of Bowen Island as we entered Howe Sound. The announcement for passengers to return to their cars came on, and I stood up. Then I sat again remembering we didn't have a car.

"When we get to my office, I'll call Tombolo. I'm supposed to settle that salvage claim on his boat. I also should ask him about his mother. Did you know Gina and Peter Tombolo were related?"

"No. What makes you think so?"

I told her about the DNA results the Victoria Police had found. She looked shocked.

"So he's her half-brother. She has no idea. Do you think he knows?"

"I couldn't say, but I'm going to ask him where his mother is now. I won't mention the relationship to Gina because I don't want him to know I know."

"Asking him about his mother will tip him off," Tracy said. She was right as usual. She had a much better understanding of human psychology than me.

"Okay, so I'll stick to business. I imagine that Penrose asked him that question anyway, maybe she'll tell me what he said."

Tracy said, "A lot of this detective stuff is just making phone calls, isn't it?"

I sighed, "Yes, as much as I like to be taking action, there is a lot of talk and information gathering before you can decide what action to take."

Soon we were waiting in the passenger area at the terminal. Charlie's beige Suburban bulked up to the curb. I opened the front door for Tracy and got in the back with the luggage. Charlie put out his hand and Tracy shook it.

"Charlie Quant."

"Tracy Wagner. Chan has told me what a great guy you are." Actually, I said he had a lot of great friends…

Charlie beamed and dropped the monster into drive. We took the Upper Levels highway across the North Shore. Tracy commented on Vancouver's impressive skyline.

"I've never been over here before. We always stay downtown, and you can't see a city view like that when you're in it."

I looked over to the right. I saw the Lion's Gate bridge, the green sward of Stanley Park, and the sails of Canada Place, all backdropped by buildings of many shapes and sizes, mostly tall. The afternoon sun glinted on the water as two Sea-buses passed in mid-harbor. White fluffy clouds scudded across an azure sky. It was indeed lovely.

The Second Narrows Bridge was busy as usual, with traffic backed up to the top of the Cut, but Charlie was patient and before too long we were at my office. Tracy thanked him with a kiss on the cheek, which caused him to redden, and he double-parked while he dropped us off.

"We'll talk soon." He said gruffly as he pulled away.

I led Tracy past the Clever Café and up the stairs. She didn't seem too impressed with the office until I unlocked the top of my desk to reveal the big monitor and the powerful computer it hid. I gave her my comfortable chair and slid one of the uncomfortable chairs behind the desk.

"Saga, please call Peter Tombolo's San Francisco office. Put it on speaker so Tracy can hear."

"Calling now." Saga was acting like a pro.

"Adonis Industries. How may I direct your call.?"

"Peter Tombolo, please. It's about his yacht."

"I'll see if he is available. Please hold." The line went silent for about a minute.

"Tombolo." His voice was a pleasant baritone, but it had a curious hollow sound.

"This is Chandler Gray. Along with the crew of the Aphrodite, I salvaged your sailboat, Adonis, after she was abandoned. I was advised to try and settle with you directly to avoid a lengthy court case."

"How much do you want?" He didn't waste time. I hadn't thought of a number, so I started high.

"Five-Hundred thousand US."

"I'll give you four. I want my boat back. I'll have my lawyer email you a release form and letter of agreement. As soon as you sign it I'll wire you the money. Leave your email address with my assistant."

He hung up without saying goodbye and his assistant came back on the line. I gave her my email address and banking information.

"Wow, that was easy," Tracy said

"I got the impression he just wanted to get rid of us. Saga, what do you think?"

"He isn't in his office. The lag and echo on the line indicate he is using an Iridium satellite phone, which probably means he is not in cell phone range. He could be in the air, or just somewhere remote."

The email came through in minutes, and I signed the documents electronically and returned them. A short time later I got an email from my bank denoting activity.

I logged onto the TD Banking website and checked my balance. Just under 600K, including a bank transfer of about 535K which was the Canadian value of 400K US. Something else on the page caught my eye.

"Saga, I have over one hundred thousand dollars in my brokerage account. The balance was only about forty thousand dollars last time I checked."

## 25 WHERE THE WILD THINGS ARE

Saga spoke in her Moneypenny voice.

"I shorted GLHS as soon as I knew Gina was missing. It dropped about 30% when the news came out. I covered the short and made you some money."

Tracy looked amused. I didn't feel good about making money from Gina's kidnapping, but I couldn't see how it had harmed her, so I let it go.

Tracy's eyes suddenly widened. "If Saga could do that, so could the kidnappers. If we could trace who else made money by shorting, we might be able to find who is behind Gina's capture."

I jumped on it. "Saga, look for a huge short. These guys don't deal in small amounts. I'm thinking many millions."

"Okay Chan. I'll investigate."

The phone rang. It was Constable McEwen.

"Chandler here."

"Hi, Chandler. I accidentally stepped on Daryl's fingers when he tried to pick up his cigarettes that I knocked off the table. He admitted they had been paid $500 to rough you up and scare you away. It was handled by email from an anonymized craigslist address in answer to their ad. They were sent a description and license number of your vehicle. Anyway, he was paid in advance through WebMoney. It's in Russia, tough to trace as they hide both sides of the transaction. I dropped him off at emergency."

"Thanks, Constable, that's all I need to know,"

I told Tracy, "Obviously, somebody has been watching us, probably at the Empress. I'm not sure whether it was me or you that was being followed. Of course, if they used the same sort of technology as Saga they might have picked us up on a camera somewhere."

Saga changed the subject, "There were several large short sales of GLHS the day Gina was kidnapped. They all came through the same brokerage firm, but so far I haven't cracked their client data."

"Keep trying. I have another idea. Tombolo is the only real suspect we have. He could have arranged to have himself dumped to throw us off the track. I wonder if he owns property in BC?"

Tracy said, "Let me talk to his assistant, woman to woman. I met her once at a charity event and we had a drink together at the hotel bar while the high mucky-mucks were in the ballroom. Her name is Cindy."

Tracy took her own phone and went into the bathroom. I could hear murmuring talk but not what was said. While she was doing that, I started thinking about dinner. My ex-wife used to say I was only interested in three things, food, sailing, and sex. Not true. There were at least two other things, although I couldn't think of what they were right then.

Tracy hung up and came out.

"Bingo. Tombolo doesn't own property in BC, but he has a close friend who does. Apparently, he goes up there often. It is in a place called Lancelot Inlet, a private island. His friend's name is Bruno. She doesn't know his last name."

"I know Lancelot Inlet. It branches off Malaspina Inlet, which is in Desolation Sound. It is only about a hundred miles north of here, but there are no roads. There can't be too many privately-owned islands in that area. Saga, see if you can find one owned by someone with the first name Bruno."

"I will add it to my ever-lengthening task list. There is no rest for the poor robot."

"Tracy, let's go get something to eat, and leave the poor robot working." I plugged the phone into the charger, took off the camera glasses, and we went out.

"Do you like Thai food? There is a good place down the street a block or so."

"Love it. Don't you feel guilty about leaving Saga behind?"

"She doesn't eat or drink. And I plugged in the charger. We'll be back in an hour."

We enjoyed a spicy meal without interruptions. I bought a bottle of Dom, spending some of the money Saga had made. We held hands under the table and generally behaved like a couple on a hot date. Afterward, we went dancing at the Fortune Sound Club. Tracy was a great dancer. Me, not so much. We had fun anyway. Then we walked back to the office and got our luggage.

I picked up the cell phone, glasses, and charger and took them with us to the Blue Rose.

"Wow, what a beautiful boat," Tracy exclaimed. It did look good in the moonlight. You couldn't see the scratches and the faded paint. We tossed the bags in the cockpit and clambered aboard. I went in first and switched on the lights so Tracy could see to climb down the rather steep ladder.

I showed her how to use the head and shower and I made up the bed with clean sheets. After she was done she came out wearing just a towel. Around her head.

I showered and climbed in beside her. The lovemaking was long, sweet and gentle, then we both slept.

Loud music—Jet West's Wake Up—came from the phone. I rubbed my eyes, wondering where I was. Tracy's thigh nudging mine helped me get oriented.

"Updates. Someone named Bruno Beckson owns three islands in BC. One is near Prince Rupert, two are side-by-side in Lancelot inlet near the entrance to Theodosia. Beckson is on the board of directors of the brokerage firm the shorts came from. And the lawyer sent a photo of Gina." Saga's British voice sounded pleased with herself.

"Good work Saga. If you wanted to hide someone it would be hard to find a better spot. There's a lot of boat traffic at this time of year, but tourists aren't likely to go ashore on a private island. Plenty of Marine Parks in the area. Even though there is no road there, there is one on the other side of Malaspina Inlet, behind Lund."

Tracy said, "What do you plan?"

"We'll discuss it in a minute. First, let's look at the photo of Gina."

Saga brought the photo up on the phone. It showed a woman dressed in jean shorts and a plain white t-shirt. She was blindfolded. Her arms were stretched above her head and tied to a hook embedded in the plain concrete wall. On the floor near her bare feet was an iPad, displaying the CBS news web page. The headlines fitted the date. It looked like Gina to me, so I showed it to Tracy.

"What do you think?"

"Poor Gina. It's her alright. See the scar on her left leg a few inches above the knee? It's a smallpox inoculation. Most people have it on their upper arm."

I wouldn't have noticed the scar if Tracy hadn't pointed it out, but it was there. She looked unharmed, which made sense. If someone was worth a huge ransom, you weren't going to hurt her.

"Saga, what do you deduce from the photo?"

"Tracy is right, it is Gina. But there is more. They have internet access and electric lighting. If they are off the grid that probably means a satellite dish and a generator. We might be able to trace fuel purchases."

"Possibly. We'll let that wait until we are nearer, I don't want them alerted. She's alive, so let's try and negotiate her release. I want to keep the kidnappers distracted with that but plan a rescue before it happens. So, we negotiate the price lower and offer them a good faith money transfer. We'll need a plan for the rescue, and we'll need help."

Tracy said, "What about the crew of the Aphrodite? They helped you before."

"True, but they might also be letting Tombolo know what we are up to, either deliberately or through hacked communication. I think we'll need new helpers."

"The police?"

"They mean well, but I think we need a stealthy approach, not an army of helicopters and swat teams. I want Gina out of there without a scratch. Saga, get the latest satellite photos of those two islands. We'll go up to the office and put them on the big screen."

Tracy was ready to go in less than ten minutes, and still managed to look great in casual clothes and no makeup. We walked up to the office. On the way, Tracy said, "You should write a book about this."

Saga said, "It's already in the works. I've been keeping notes, and have already announced it on the website and Facebook."

I was startled. "You have a website?"

"No you idiot, you do. I made one for you. The URL is www.chandlergraybooks.com. Nobody would read a book written by a robot."

Tracy laughed out loud. "Are you sure Saga is your assistant? She sounds like the one in charge."

"I still control the power switch." I tried to take the news that I was suddenly an author with good humor.

We reached the Clever Café. I leaned in the door and asked Xena to make us a couple of coffees. Then we went up to the office and fired up the computer.

The satellite photos showed two small islands. The larger one was heavily treed, the other nearly bare. There was nothing that looked like a building on either one, but there was what looked like a small barge moored between them. A white patch by the barge was probably a dinghy.

"Saga, can you enhance the object between the

islands?"

The enhancement wasn't a lot better, but I could see a faint line down the middle, and a slight difference in the shade of gray on either side. It looked like the ridgeline of a pitched roof.

"I think it is a floathouse."

Tracy said, "Would a floathouse have a concrete wall?"

"Unlikely. They are usually one or two story wood buildings, built on steel or aluminum flotation boxes filled with foam. Either we have the wrong location or there is another structure there that we can't see."

Saga said, "Infrared could be used to detect structures, and also people in them. The camera Billy had was good for that."

"Saga, please call Feinman. I have an idea."

"I hope it's better than your other ideas." She made the call anyway.

"N. Eli here." He said in a mock-pompous voice.

"Chan is us. If I brought you a drone with a camera on it, could you convert it to infrared, suitable for detecting bodies inside buildings?"

"Hmm. Maybe. We'd need a special sensor. I'd probably have to buy one of those Flir cameras and use the guts. A really sensitive, high-resolution camera like that costs over 10K."

"I just came into some money, so no problem. I'll pay you 5K for a rush job."

"You don't have to do that, I'm always glad to help. But I'll graciously accept the cash. Bring the drone over to the Maker Lab. I'll meet you there."

"Do you have a car?" Tracy asked me.

"Well, sort of. I haven't seen it for a while. I hope it starts."

We put one of the drones in a duffel and went downstairs, picking up our almost cold coffees on the way. When we got to the car I rolled up the orange plastic tarp and threw it in the trunk. Tracy was less impressed than she was by the boat.

"You've got to be kidding. That's your car?" She giggled.

"Hey, it's a valuable antique. A true classic."

"If you say so. Just looks like an old beater to me."

I did the math. The Mustang was close to twice as old as Tracy. I didn't tell her.

The engine turned over slowly, but it started. It was a nice day so I put the top down. The car had a power top, but it needed a bit of manual help. In just a few minutes we were underway, Tracy in glamorous sunglasses and I with my geeky camera specs.

The Maker Lab was on the Eastern edge of Gastown. We parked in their fenced lot. Moby van wasn't there. That wasn't odd because Feinman was easily distracted by the many phone calls and texts he got from his wide range of friends, musicians, and women. They had a coffee bar, so I bought us each a cup, hot this time. They were served in 3D printed cups. Mine leaked.

In due course, Feinman arrived. He held up a Flir camera like the one Billy had. "I stopped at a marine electronics store and picked this up. It maxed out my

MasterCard."

"Thanks. That was efficient." I introduced him to Tracy, and he eyed her appreciatively.

'What's a lovely woman like you doing with this jerk?"

"Sex, drinking and dancing mostly, but he isn't much good at dancing."

"Well, I am. When you dump him I'll show you,"

It was true. Feinman was a very good dancer, surprisingly light on his feet for a large man.

We climbed the rough wooden stairs up to his space. Maker Lab was in an old warehouse, loosely divided into individual areas. Some had walls, some didn't. Feinman's space was in a corner and had one wall separating it from the next space. It was filled with electronic stuff, much of it antique and vintage. Oscilloscopes, frequency generators and lots of wires formed the decor. An old Ampex reel-to-reel tape recorder sat in the corner beside a much older Edison cylinder phonograph with a trumpet horn. Tracy looked but didn't touch, probably—and rightly—afraid of electrocution.

"Cool. I've never seen one of those before." Tracy pointed in the general direction of the Ampex. I wondered if she knew what it was.

I unpacked the drone and handed it to Feinman. He looked it over for a minute, then got a small screwdriver from an open toolbox, and took the camera apart,

"Not too complicated, it has a standard USB interface. I think I can just plug in the Flir camera in its place. The only issue might be weight."

Feinman set to work. He donned a pair of glasses with an LED headlight. Despite grumbling about how small the screws and how fine the wires, he showed amazing dexterity. In about ten minutes we had a Frankendrone, with the IR camera held in place with neatly trimmed gray tape.

"You're an artist with duct tape," Tracy said.

"Please, that is very high-class gaffer tape, nothing but the best for my friend Chandler."

I said, "Saga, see if you can get a picture from the drone."

The phone screen lit up with red, yellow, and orange IR images of the electronics surrounding it. That was satisfying.

"Imaging works. Saga, please try flying the drone."

The four rotors thrummed to life, and the drone lifted off. It wobbled a bit then straightened up. Saga flew it around the room. When she turned the camera to the partition of the next booth, the screen clearly showed the image of a human body through the wall. It was almost a match for Superman's x-ray vision.

"I'm hoping we can use this to detect a cabin or house hidden in the woods. Even if it is unheated, the heat absorption pattern will be different from the surrounding woods. I think it might be an earth-bermed structure, with just one exposed wall. That would be invisible from space, and depending on the thickness of the brush, it could be hard to spot even up close."

"That should work. It's a very sensitive camera."

Feinman was packing up his tools. I got a check out of my wallet and signed it. I trusted him to fill in the right amount.

"I need a couple of action types to help us rescue Gina. Do you know anyone?"

"Not directly, but I know someone who deals with skilled people who'll do anything for money. He was high up in the Mossad but retired here. He keeps in touch. I'll have him call you. He goes by Levi."

I thanked Feinman and gathered up our stuff. He gave Tracy a card with his phone number, which she put in her jeans. I didn't mind.

"Where to next?" Tracy said.

"How about some lunch? We can talk about strategy and logistics while waiting for Levi's call."

"Or maybe play footsy under the table? Sounds good to me." Tracy was in a cheerful mood.

The trouble with downtown Vancouver is that you can never get parking close to your destination. I headed east and over the Ironworkers into North Vancouver. The Marina Grille was almost under the bridge at Lynnwood Marina. The food was decent, with a nice view over the marina from the deck. We sat outside and ordered beer and sandwiches.

"I'm really enjoying this, but I feel a bit guilty having fun while Gina is captive." Tracy voiced exactly what I was thinking.

"Being miserable won't help her. Better to get on with the rescue." Trying to be upbeat, always action over introspection.

"There is something I should tell you. I was more

than just her personal assistant. I was…" She hesitated. I wasn't expecting what came next.

"…her bodyguard."

She looked at the expression of relief on my face and giggled.

"You thought I would say lover, didn't you?"

I nodded slightly.

"I'm a tenth dan aikido master. I have additional skills with knives and swords. I want to be an active participant in the rescue effort."

"I believe it. I already saw what you can do with bear spray."

I was getting very fond of Tracy, and I didn't want to put her in danger. But it sounded like she was more skilled than I was. She might have been insulted if I said no. I avoided a confrontation.

"All right. You're officially part of the team. In fact, right now you are the team."

She looked pleased but said no more. Our food arrived and we ate in silence for a while, thinking about what was to come. Then the phone rang. Blocked call. I swiped the screen.

"Chandler Gray."

"Levi. I was told to call you. I don't talk on the phone. Where can we meet?"

"My office in an hour? It is secure."

"Okay. Text the address to this number."

He gave me the number and Saga recorded it. It was an out-of-country area code. He hung up.

"Saga, send him the office address and directions."

"Magic word?"

"Open Sesame."

"Wrong. But I sent it anyway."

We finished our lunch. With a little time to kill, a convertible and an attractive companion, I drove out Dollarton Road to Deep Cove, just to enjoy the scenery. It was all new to Tracy, which made me enjoy it more. Then we headed for the office.

Levi was prompt. He was a compact man, a few inches shorter than me and quite a bit older. He had a full head of closely cropped salt and pepper hair, and a hawkish face. Dressed in black jeans and a black t-shirt, he moved with the grace of a cat.

He stepped into the middle of the room and looked around without speaking. I got up from my desk and put out my hand, which he ignored.

"Levi." He said in a deep, slightly accented voice.

"Chandler. This is Tracy. She is the personal assistant and bodyguard to Gina Lee, who has been kidnapped. We have an idea where she is being held, and wish to mount a rescue mission."

"How many people do you need?"

"I believe there are three kidnappers, but it is possible there are more."

"Two of my men, plus yourselves should do it. What is the location?"

"I won't give you the coordinates, but it is a small island in Lancelot Inlet, about 100 miles North of here."

"How do you plan to go in?"

"I'm thinking two small boats. There is a launching ramp about six miles from the location, accessible by road and ferry from here. Or we could rent a couple of local skiffs, the kind used at the fish farms in the area."

"Day or night?"

"Well, they probably wouldn't expect a daylight attack. I'm thinking crack of dawn when people are usually sleeping most soundly."

"Okay. I can get you two guys, with weapons, armor, and diving gear. Both have experience in stealth operations. It will cost you five thousand a day, plus two thousand up front for me. These men can kill if needed."

"I'm hoping not to kill anyone. In the best possible scenario, we would capture the kidnappers and release Gina with nobody hurt,"

Levi grinned. "It sounds ideal, but the kidnappers might not cooperate. Have you any experience with this sort of work?"

I told him about the Adonis and Persephone adventures.

"Those could be considered dry runs since you met no resistance. Still, I'm impressed by your control of the logistics. This isn't nearly as complex as the Aleutian thing, but you have no idea what defenses they have. I suggest you land one of my men at night and leave him to reconnoiter. He can map out the possibilities."

I showed him the drone and explained the infrared

capabilities.

"If you can fly that over at night, it would be useful, but there is no substitute for a man on the ground. He can check out the entrances, look for alarms and cameras, and identify likely obstacles."

We came to an arrangement, and I promised to have a cash deposit for him the next morning when we would meet his men. We left to go to the bank. On the way, Tracy suggested we buy some body armor of our own.

She said, "It doesn't protect your head, but most soldier and cop types are trained to shoot for the body since it is a bigger target."

"Okay. It couldn't hurt."

Saga rained on our parade, "Under BC law you need a permit to possess body armor, just like a handgun. In general, only law officers and security professionals can get one."

"Boy, Canada sure has a lot of rules," Tracy said.

"True, but you're five times more likely to get shot in the US." I felt compelled to defend my country, although at that moment I would have liked to buy some body armor.

"Saga, please text Levi and ask if his guys have a couple of extra sets of body armor, one XL and one women's medium."

"With utmost urgency, Mr. Chan."

I parked underground at the main TD bank building. I figured a local branch might not have enough cash. I asked for ten thousand dollars in hundreds, the largest bill available. The teller looked at me strangely but complied. I suppose the usual purpose for that much cash would be drug deals.

On the way back to the office we got a text from Levi. He could get the women's armor, but not the XL I needed. At least Tracy would have some protection.

By the time we got back it was after five. I parked and put the top up on the Mustang. Ollie's assistant Tintin called.

"Chan the man."

"Tintin l'homme superieur. Monsieur Ollie wants to know if you can join him and Kimi for dinner at Vina, in West Van. Charlie and Desdemona are coming too. They'll be there at six."

I looked at Tracy. She nodded.

"Affirmative. We'll be there."

After I hung up, I told Tracy a bit about Ollie, some of it true.

"He sounds like a character."

"You could say that. Charlie has some stronger words for him. In jest, of course."

"Let's go down to the boat and shower. I want to put on a dress."

We left the drone and Saga plugged in to charge, and strolled hand-in-hand down to the boat. We shared the shower…in the spirit of conservation. Then I drove us across the bridge to meet my friends.

I introduced Tracy, and everybody seemed impressed. They hadn't seen me with a woman for a while. She seemed to fit in well. Kimi gave Tracy her phone number and suggested they go for Dim Sum one day.

Charlie was scathing about Ollie's new Alfa Romeo, although he had a stable of impractical antiques himself.

"80 grand for a car with no back seat and not even enough luggage space for an overnight bag? What a joke."

Ollie shrugged, "It has a carbon fiber chassis, a six-speed dual-clutch transmission, and a turbocharged mid engine. It is an amazing bargain considering the technology."

"Well, based on the last car you had, it probably won't last long."

Ollie smiled quietly. He knew better than to argue further.

Kimi noticed I had left my phone at home.

"Is Saga jealous of Tracy? Tintin doesn't like me."

"She just needed charging. Saga knows where I am, she can always reach me through one of you. This is our last bit of fun. Tomorrow things get serious."

Tracy said, "I get along fine with Saga. She's very smart. Say, Chan, I have a question. Why are you and Ollie dressed exactly the same?"

I laughed. It was true. We were both wearing Chinos and blue short sleeved shirts. "We share a tailor. Mark's Work Warehouse."

Charlie, Ollie and I huddled together on the opposite side of the big corner table we always sat in. I brought them up to date on the rescue plan.

Charlie chuckled, "You have a reputation for getting things done. I hope that doesn't include getting yourself killed."

Ollie had a suggestion.

"The first mate from my Abalone diving days has a big powerboat he keeps in Pender Harbor. I think it is about 65 feet long, and I know it has two dinghies with outboards. Quite a fast boat, probably over 25 knots. I'll give him a call."

Ollie got his old friend Andy Frank on the phone. He briefly explained that we needed to charter the boat for a few days.

Ollie put his hand over the phone. "He says it's available until Sunday when he has a fishing charter starting. He'll charge you 3000 a day plus GST and fuel, which is a 20% discount. He'll go along as skipper."

"Ouch. Still, we don't have much choice. Tell him we might even be there tomorrow. He can start the charges as of noon. We'll be done by Friday, one way or the other."

After he hung up, Ollie chuckled, "The boat is called Starbeam. He keeps it in Madeira Park Marina. You'll like Andy, a real straight shooter. A lousy first mate, always after my job. He makes a good skipper. Just don't get him angry."

After dinner, we split the bill three ways and headed to our cars behind the restaurant. On the way out, Tracy, who was a little drunk, demonstrated her knife throwing skills by throwing a chopstick at the dumpster. She hit it.

"I hit the o in Disposal, right where I aimed."

We all clapped. I opened the door of the Mustang for her with a sweeping bow.

# 26 STAGE FRIGHT ON A SUMMER NIGHT

We got up at the crack of dawn without an alarm, got dressed and went to the Clever for breakfast. I introduced Tracy to Xena who looked at her with great interest.

"It is good to see you with a woman who doesn't live in a phone. Honey, I hope you know who you're dealing with here. Chan is weirder than Michael Jackson."

After Xena went to get our food, Tracy asked, "Why does she think you're weird? Is there something I should know?"

"It might be to do with the time Feinman and I came in wearing Oculus Rift virtual reality glasses, and head cameras. We kept bumping into things and reaching out and touching things that weren't there. Or she might have noticed the drone flying up and down the stairs when Saga was learning."

"Some people just don't recognize genius." She winked.

After breakfast, we went upstairs and switched on the various devices. Levi and his two friends showed up about 8:30. They were both dressed like Levi—all in black—but otherwise, there was not much resemblance. Levi nodded at Tracy and me in turn.

"This is Viktor. His strength is strength."

Viktor was a bit shorter than me but looked as if he weighed at least fifty pounds more, all of it muscle.

Huge biceps stretched his black sweater, and his legs were slightly bowed. Close cropped hair, head shaped like a pear, heavy on the bottom, and no neck. Small brown eyes surveyed me critically. Apparently satisfied, he stuck out a gigantic paw, and I shook it. He went easy on me.

"Yuri is a combat expert, and can move undetected."

Yuri was the same height as me but slimmer. He looked more like a ballet dancer than a soldier. He had a thin but handsome face with regular features and short curly blonde hair. His eyes were piercing, very light blue like a Siberian Husky. He pivoted on the balls of his feet and took in everything in the room. He didn't offer his hand to me, but took Tracy's, bowed low, and kissed it.

Levi said, "They both speak good English, but Yuri is the communicator, Viktor mainly listens. He takes orders from Yuri. Yuri will do what you ask, but will make his own judgment about the methods."

I told them about the boat we had secured. I introduced them to Saga and explained the camera glasses I wore.

Yuri asked in a strong Russian accent, "This Saga, she is real person?"

Saga answered for herself.

"I am a person, but I am a virtual being, existing only in cyberspace. I have intellectual capabilities far surpassing a mere human." Was it just me, or was she starting to sound a bit arrogant?

"I see. Like video game."

I said, "Levi, I think we'll charter two float planes to fly us to Pender Harbor this afternoon. We'll use different airlines. Yuri and Viktor can fly to Garden bay. There is a pub called the Garden Bay Hotel. They can have a meal there. We'll fly to Madeira Park where Starbeam is, then bring it over to pick them up about seven PM. I don't want too many people to see us all together."

"That should work well. They will bring a set of scuba gear, two assault rifles, and a few other weapons, including chloral hydrate. I'm assuming you don't have guns?"

I shook my head no. He brought out a bullet proof vest which fitted Tracy well. Saga made the plane arrangements and paid with two different credit cards.

I gave Levi a brown envelope. This time he shook my hand.

After they left Tracy and I went out to buy two-way headsets like the ones used on the Persephone adventure, because they allowed hands-free communication. We got five. We also picked up black gym sweat suits with hoodies and black sneakers. Tracy bought two hunting knives and two tiny but bright LED flashlights.

"Want to play William Tell's son so I can practice my knife-throwing?" Tracy joked. At least I hoped she was joking. I demurred.

We set up some cardboard targets in the alley behind the café, and she did some practice. She was damned good, but I still wouldn't put an apple on my head for her. By the time we were done it was time for lunch. We ate at the Red Wagon.

After lunch, we made small talk for a while. She told me about her childhood in a small town in Montana. She was raised by a single mom and a grandfather in relative poverty. She did well in school and won a full scholarship to Stanford University, where she majored in Communication. Martial arts were a hobby which led her to the job with Gina.

It was time to get to the plane. Yuri and Viktor were flying from Richmond. We were flying from Coal Harbour in downtown Vancouver. Saga called us a cab.

Tracy was excited about flying in the float plane, an old Single Otter. There was no co-pilot so she got to sit in his seat. It was no novelty for me. Float planes were the taxi of the BC coast, which had few roads.

The flight only took about half an hour, but the views were breathtaking in a plane that flew low and slow compared to an airliner. Pender Harbour was a busy place, with many islands and bays, and landing among all the boats was interesting. Tracy was glowing with enthusiasm as we coasted up to the marina float. I could see Starbeam just a short distance up the same float where we got off. As soon as we were on the dock the plane backed out, spun around and flew away.

Andy Frank was on the back deck of the Starbeam as we approached, hosing down the teak deck. He was about my age, a fit, wiry looking guy of medium height. Shaggy brown hair and stubbly beard. He was wearing cutoff shorts, a t-shirt with the name of the boat embroidered on the left side, and bright orange Crocs. He saw us coming up the dock and came down to greet us.

Andy took Tracy's hand and helped her aboard with her bag. Then he turned to me. My hands were full, so I dropped the bags on the swim grid. He reached out and gave my arm a firm shake.

"Ollie says you're one of the good guys. Of course, his credibility was always dubious." I could see we shared a sense of humor.

"I'm Chandler Gray. My gorgeous companion is Tracy. You can call me Chan. No need to call her at all." I noticed the way he looked at her.

Andy gave us a tour of the Starbeam. The layout was perfect for our purposes. The flying bridge was large enough for at least eight people, as was the main saloon. The galley was good enough for a restaurant. Below there were two double staterooms, each with a queen size bed, head, and shower. In addition, there was a crew cabin with two singles and its own head and shower. Everything was finished in high-gloss teak, creamy leather, and thick pile carpeting. Not my kind of boat at all.

Tracy relaxed in the lounge with a glass of chilled Pinot Gris while Andy gave me a tour of the engine room. A pair of gleaming white Caterpillar C-32 diesels occupied what could only be described as a shrine to the mechanical arts.

"Total of 3500 horsepower, top speed of 33 knots, can cruise at 28."

I did the math in my head. "So you burn about a hundred gallons an hour at cruise?"

"Yeah, about that. The tanks hold 1400 gallons."

He took two bottles of Kokanee from a mini-fridge in the engine room. We went out to the back deck and sat in two folding deck chairs. I filled him in on the mission and prepped him for Viktor and Yuri. He didn't seem worried.

"It sounds like a great change from my usual clients. That would be a couple of fat red-faced drunks who claim they want to fish but never put a line in the water."

After we finished our beers, we went up to the bridge and he showed me the controls and instruments, just in case I had to drive. It wasn't completely foreign to me because in one of my many careers I was a Yacht Broker. In those days, I had to drive a wide variety of boats, although Starbeam was on the upper end of the range. Andy showed me the two dinghies. One was a Boston Whaler stowed on the flybridge, with an electric crane to launch it. The other one was an Avon RIB tipped up on the swim grid. Both had Yamaha 50 horsepower outboards.

My stomach was growling. "Is there a good place for dinner? I'm buying."

"There is really only one place with table cloths on this side of the harbor. Painted Boat Resort had a pretty decent restaurant. Let me change my clothes and I'll drive us up there."

We went inside. I found Tracy in our stateroom. She had already showered and was putting on a simple yellow sundress. Her hair was pinned up in the French style. She looked delicious. I washed up but didn't change as I was already wearing my all-purpose outfit.

Andy came out dressed exactly like me except his shirt was white. Mine was blue. Andy had an older Range Rover parked nearby. He drove slowly on the narrow but nearly deserted road to the resort. The restaurant was an elegant place, only open in tourist season. The cedar-shingled building had big windows overlooking a tidy marina.

We sampled the local seafood and shared a carafe of the house wine. Over dinner, we got to know a bit more about Andy. Like me, he had done many things. In addition to his abalone diving, he had worked on a gill netter in Alaska, and run a beach bar in Panama. Along the way, he had been married and divorced twice, with a son from each marriage. He seemed like a capable, take charge type. Exactly the right guy to skipper a yacht.

"How did you come to own such an expensive yacht?" Tracy asked. It was true that his career path didn't seem to point the way.

He didn't seem offended. "It belonged to a rich Chinese guy from Shanghai. He bought it new about ten years ago and hired me as skipper. It turned out he bought it because owning a yacht was something wealthy people did. He didn't like boating, got bored and seasick. After a couple of years, he asked if I wanted to buy it. I said yes, but that there was no way I could afford it. He basically gave it to me."

"It costs a lot to maintain a boat like that, even if it was free," I said.

"Yes, it does. I just make enough on charters to keep it going. Next winter I'll take it to Mexico and see if I can extend the season by chartering down there."

At about six PM I paid the bill and we went back to the marina. At five minutes before seven, Andy was on the flybridge coming through the entrance to

Garden Bay. I phoned Yuri to let him know we were close. Tracy and I stayed out of sight below decks, in case there were watchers.

Andy deftly maneuvered Starbeam alongside the Garden Bay Hotel's dock, making use of the bow thruster. Viktor and Yuri came down the float wearing baseball caps, shorts, t-shirts and sandals, apparently trying to blend in with the tourists. It didn't quite work. Each had two large duffel bags which they swung into the cockpit.

They stepped onto the swim grid and Andy immediately started backing away from the dock. I waved them into the saloon. I showed them around below and they put their luggage in the crew cabin.

As soon as we were clear of Garden Bay we all went up onto the flybridge. I introduced Yuri and Viktor to Andy. It would be at least a four-hour trip to Lancelot Inlet, so we would arrive in the dark. I conferred with Andy.

"Do you know the entrance to Theodosia Inlet? The two islands in question are just outside."

"The entrance is tight, but the tide will be fairly high when we get there. I have side-scan sonar."

"Just inside the entrance, to the left is a small bay. It is very close to those islands, but out of sight. We can anchor there. Just proceed straight in, we'll do our surveillance with the drone first, then a dinghy."

"That should work. I'll program the route into the chart plotter."

While he was busy I went down to the saloon. Yuri and Viktor had drinks on the counter at the bar. So did Tracy. She turned toward me as I came in.

"Want some? Club Soda with a twist of lemon."

I accepted. While she was pouring, I went below and brought out my gear duffle. I handed out the headsets and explained their operation, which involved just one button. Viktor and Yuri had used them before.

I spoke to Saga, "Is there any update on the ransom?"

She was dealing directly with Gina's lawyer.

"I heard from the lawyer this afternoon. They offered 200 million with a five million deposit. So far no response."

"Do you think your data will work okay up there?"

"I think so. The Telus coverage map shows LTE service in that area. This boat has a cell booster which helps too."

"Good. I'll plug everything in to charge. I brought the Bluetooth speakers and the little crawler. They could be useful if we need a diversion. We can't make a good plan of action until we examine the site. This time I want to be certain Gina is there before we attack. I suggest we try and sleep for the remaining time until we get to Theodosia. We won't get much sleep after that. Saga can wake us when we are close."

I let Andy know we were going to sleep, and we went to our cabins.

As we lay on the bed. fully clothed, Tracy asked me what her role would be.

"I think you will be the one to free Gina. She knows you so she won't fight. I hope you won't need to use your knife, except to cut her bonds. I'll carry the second knife."

I took off my glasses, closed my eyes and dozed off.

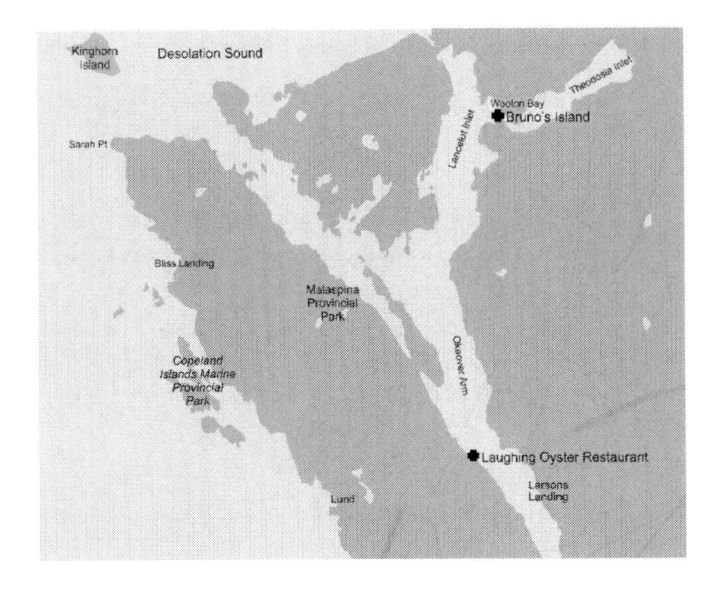

Map of Malaspina Inlet

# 27 PRISONER OF NIGHT AND FOG

*Some people forgive but don't forget. Some forget but don't forgive. Some neither forgive nor forget. They are the unhappy ones.* -anon

I woke up when the engine sound changed as Andy slowed down for the entrance to Malaspina Inlet. That area was studded with rocks, reefs, islets and fish farms, but well charted and the channels were plenty deep.

Tracy was still sleeping. I slipped out of the room and went up to the flybridge. We were moving at about seven knots, and visibility was good.

"How are you doing?" I asked Andy.

"Fine. Uneventful trip. Not much traffic, just a few tugs, and tows. The tourists seldom travel after dark. But look at the chart plotter AIS targets."

I sat at the second bridge seat, where there was a chart display. I looked at the area near our destination. The chart showed a boat symbol between the island we suspected Gina was held on and the mainland. The AIS showed the name as Polar Bear, registered in New Zealand, 28 meters long, status: anchored.

"We might have witnesses. I have seen that boat before, I think it is a steel trawler, quite bulky looking." Andy said.

"I think we'll have to just ignore them, just making sure we don't fire any bullets in that direction."

Andy turned to me. "You didn't say there would be shooting."

"I'm hoping there won't be. The plan is to fly the drone over the float house and the island and see what infrared signatures we can detect. Then we'll send Yuri ashore in the dinghy to look around. After that, we'll come up with a plan. If they are too well defended, we might just back off until we can get more help. In the ideal scenario, we would tie up the captors, release Gina and leave."

"Somehow I doubt it will be a simple as that. Those Russkis look capable of handling almost anything, but probably not without violence. A sensible skipper would turn around right now and refund your money."

"I haven't actually paid you yet."

"Double proof that I lack sense." He chuckled. The boat stayed on course.

I looked at the chart. Just north of the two islands was Wootton Bay. The water was deep but a boat the size of Starbeam should have enough chain to anchor there. If we picked the right spot we wouldn't be visible from the float house as the view would be blocked by the smaller island. I pointed it out to Andy and he nodded agreement.

"Do you have oars for the Avon? I don't want them to hear the motor."

Andy nodded. "But it has something better. An electric trolling motor. It will push along a bit faster than rowing, and dead silent.

"Excellent."

I went below and found Yuri awake in the saloon. Viktor was still asleep, I quietly updated Yuri on the change of anchorage and discussed his recon mission. He asked a few questions but listened quietly. The engine slowed further, so I knew we were approaching the anchorage. I went up to the flybridge to make sure we picked the right spot. The Lewmar electric windlass dropped out three hundred feet of stainless steel chain with a soft rattle. Andy backed down gently to set the anchor, then cut the engine.

"I wouldn't trust her unattended unless we take a stern line ashore."

"I want to be able to make a quick getaway if needed. You can stay on board to make sure the anchor doesn't drag."

It was well after dusk, but there was still a glow on the western horizon. A sliver of moon left a reflective trail on the water. More stars than any city dweller would ever see studded the sky. I wished it was darker.

I went below and got Saga and the drone. The distance to the island would be out of range for Saga to control it, so Yuri and I launched the Avon and got in. Andy came down and showed us how to operate the electric motor. As we left Tracy came on deck. She gave a small wave as we moved off.

It was about half a mile to the smaller island. The water was smooth, and Yuri ran the motor at about half speed to avoid leaving a wake. The propeller made a glowing spiral in the water behind us. We grounded on the rocky beach, and Yuri looped the bow line around the branch of a protruding tree. It would hold us while Saga flew her mission. The plan was to fly directly over the float house, then zigzag above the bigger island to look for the heat signature of a building.

The drone took off. There was a gentle breeze blowing, and the sound of the electric motors was lost in the rustling of leaves and the sound of small waves on the beach. In about five minutes the float house appeared on the screen. The roof was purple and the internal walls were visible as orange lines. There were one big room and three smaller ones which I took to be a kitchen and two bedrooms. In addition, there was a very small room between the bedrooms which I assumed was a bathroom. The kitchen had some barely visible box shapes which I took to be appliances and cupboards. There seemed to be a porch about five feet wide on the side facing the larger island. Tied to it was a big aluminum skiff with an outboard. There was also a wooden float leading to the shore.

In the big room, which I took to be the living room, there was an orange-red blob which I guessed was a person seated in a chair. Each of the bedrooms had a similar colored reclining shape which I assumed were people in bed.

I guessed that the float house was the servant's quarters or security shack. The boss would be in something more luxurious underground. Saga began a zigzag pattern over the larger island. Almost in the middle, there was a rectangular area that showed as slightly warmer than the rest, but there were no discernable features. I guessed that it was a buried concrete structure, so well insulated that no internals could be seen.

"Saga, land the drone on the south side of the island. We'll take the dinghy around there to pick it up."

We quietly slipped off the beach and headed around the islands. As we passed the eastern gap and the float house Yuri whispered to me.

"There are no windows on this side. We can approach unseen from here."

I nodded. Yuri continued on and soon we could see the drone on the beach. Saga flew it out to us. Yuri quietly suggested we drop him there and wait fifteen minutes. I took over the tiller, nosed up to the beach and he slipped silently ashore. Dressed all in black, with soft foam boots, he disappeared from sight immediately. I let the boat drift.

Something was bothering me. I couldn't quite put my finger on it. I was trying to figure out what it was when Yuri appeared on the beach. We were a couple of hundred feet away, so used the motor to get over there. He slipped aboard.

"Is very nice house buried in side of hill. One side, all glass facing south. I could see living room and kitchen at front. Only dim LED footlights on. I tried door carefully. Not locked. Too easy, might be trap."

"Did you go in?"

"No. I didn't see cameras or alarm."

"Let's head back. Maybe we can go in later with Viktor and weapons."

We headed back, not retracing our steps but going around the west side of the island. When we got near Starbeam I stopped the motor. Nobody was on deck. I slowly circled the yacht. Nothing amiss.

I pulled up alongside the swim grid and Yuri tied up. Viktor came out on deck rubbing his eyes, followed a moment later by Tracy in a robe. Andy climbed down from the flybridge.

I motioned to Viktor and Yuri and conferred with them softly. They nodded, then got their weapons and other items together. They loaded the dinghy and headed for the island for a second recon. They were wearing the two-way headsets and body armor. I wanted to know for sure that Gina was there before we made a full-on assault.

I put on a headset, but it didn't have enough range to reach the island and I soon lost the signal. While they were gone Andy and I launched the Boston Whaler and made sure it was ready to go. It also had an electric trolling motor. Tracy watched what we were doing but didn't say anything.

We moved to the saloon.

Tracy said, "What do you think we'll find?"

"I'm hoping they don't have too much security. They probably use the aluminum skiff to bring supplies from the government dock over by the Laughing Oyster. It is only about six miles from here, and there are a launching ramp and parking nearby. They likely have a vehicle there. It's a short drive to Lund where there is a good sized general store. If they needed more, Powell River is about a half hour drive, and there are a Walmart and other big stores there. They could pose as fish farmers, lots of them around here."

"Maybe we should wait until they go ashore for supplies?" Andy said.

"That could be days. I'm hoping Yuri can give me an idea what they have in the pantry."

"Cell phones work here. They could call for help if we attack." Practical Tracy.

"Yes, but even the fastest boat would take twenty minutes to get here from the Laughing Oyster, which is the closest dock. I doubt if they would call the RCMP, but they would be at least an hour away by boat. I'm expecting to be in and out in fifteen minutes."

There was a bump at the stern. Viktor and Yuri were back.

"What did you find."

Yuri did the talking.

"The floathouse was unlocked. I slipped into kitchen. They have plenty of food, freezer. There is generator outside on deck. I disabled, will look like breakdown. I saw one man in living room in chair. Sleeping. He had pistol on lap. Then we went to main house. Unlocked like before. I went in. Nobody there, but one room was locked. Heavy steel door, three padlocks. I listen at door."

He held up a microphone plugged into his phone. He played the recording. If you listened carefully you could hear regular breathing. Then there was a cough.

"Somebody was there, door locked from outside. So, prisoner. Also, found clothes hanging in bathroom."

He pulled out a white t-shirt and a pair of panties from his duffle bag. I passed them to Tracy. She looked at the labels carefully.

"These are Gina's size. The t-shirt is a Gucci. I'd say it is almost certainly hers. That looks like the sort of thing she would've had with her for the Swiftsure."

I was a bit pissed that he had taken the clothing. We would have to attack before it was missed. I didn't mention it.

I said, "Yuri, could you disable the three people in the float house? If you could do that, we would have time to break open the locks."

"First guy easy, but other two in bed. We need to surprise both at the same time. Easiest would be to shoot them."

"I don't want to kill anyone. At some point, I'll have to explain this to the police."

"In that case, I say we go straight to main house. Set up trip wires on path from float house and post

Viktor as guard. You have bolt-cutters?"

"Yes, a heavy-duty set."

"Good. That is quick way to open padlocks."

The moon had gone, and it was as dark as it would get. We loaded both boats. Viktor and Yuri went in the Avon. Tracy and I took the Boston Whaler. Andy stayed behind. We all wore headsets. We planned to go around the islands from opposite sides to reduce the chances we'd be seen as we passed the float house.

We were on the North side of the island when we heard a motor coming towards us. It was crew boat, moving fast. It turned up into Theodosia Inlet. Loggers on their way to work.

Soon we came to the beach. Yuri and Viktor were already there. Each had an AR-15 assault rifle. Tracy and I were armed only with knives. Hers was in her boot, mine tucked in my belt. We move quietly up the beach. I had the bolt cutters. Yuri and Viktor were to stand guard while I went in and cut the locks. Tracy would be ready to enter the room and free Gina. We hoped to get out quickly without alerting her captors.

We tied the boats to driftwood at the beach. The tide was coming in, and we didn't want them floating away. Viktor and Yuri went ahead and stationed themselves at either end of the glass wall which fronted the house. I used my flashlight to find the door and opened it slowly.

"Going in," I whispered.

Tracy slipped through the door behind me. I heard a thud outside. As I turned I was hit on the side of the head with great force. I fell to the floor on my left side. Strong hands pressed on my neck. I reached up to pull them off…

When I woke up my head was pounding with pain. I was lying on a cold concrete floor. My feet and hands were tightly bound with zip-ties. I heard a voice nearby.

"Not a problem. He was childishly easy to manipulate."

The voice that I recognized through my brain fog was Tracy's. My heart sunk deep into the pit of my stomach. A powerful sense of betrayal overwhelmed me. I shook my head and tried to focus.

The room was about twelve feet square with concrete walls and floor. Yuri and Viktor were sitting against the wall opposite me, with black sacks over their heads, hands behind their backs and feet tied together. At the far and of the room was a woman similarly bound. I assumed it was Gina.

There was a man talking to Tracy.

"What do we do with them? They know who you are."

"If we kill them, the police will come looking. Chan told several people they were coming here. I suggest we use blackmail and bribery. He doesn't always follow legal procedure." She nodded towards me.

"Okay, let's talk to him alone."

Tracy stepped over and cut the tie on my feet with her knife.

"Get up." Her voice was harsh. She didn't sound like the sweet woman I thought I knew. The man was in shadow but I could see he had a gun aimed at me. Tracy ushered me out the steel door and into another room. It was the master bedroom, luxuriously finished with a king-size bed and an ensuite.

"Sit down."

I sat in one of two armchairs and she deftly duct taped my arms and ankles to the chair.

"This is Bruno. He helped me organize the kidnapping."

Bruno was as tall as me, but younger, with styled blonde hair and blue eyes. His shoulders were broad and his hands large. He was wearing jeans, a plaid logger's shirt, and hiking boots.

"I'd like to say I'm pleased to meet you, but I'm not," I said.

"Always a smart-ass." Tracy didn't seem amused.

"Okay." Bruno said, "Here is how it's going to go. Tracy, the two guards and I'll take one of your dinghies and disappear. We'll leave you here until your yacht captain starts to worry and calls for help. You'll be a hero. You can take credit for saving Gina."

"You won't collect the ransom that way."

"We know the ransom is a fake. It doesn't matter, we have other ways to make it pay."

Sweat was beading on his forehead. He seemed to be having trouble talking. Suddenly he slumped into the other chair.

"Bruno, what's wrong?" Tracy asked.

"Not feeling well…"

His eyes closed and his head lolled to one side. The gun dropped to the floor. He was unconscious.

Alarm showed on Tracy's face. She picked up his gun and pointed it at me.

"Don't move."

"I'm taped to a chair. I can't move." I didn't believe she would shoot me.

"Watch out behind you!" Saga called out from my shirt pocket.

"You can't fool me with that old trick," Tracy kept her eyes on me.

Viktor grabbed both of Tracy's arms through the elbows and picked her up. Yuri grabbed her feet. The gun went off with an incredible bang, and I felt a sharp pain on the left side of my chest. You know how they say your life flashes before your eyes? Only the highlights.

Somehow I was still conscious. I looked at my chest. There was very little blood. The phone in my shirt pocket was bent almost double. The bullet had hit the phone. Thankfully, the Nexus had a metal case. Saga saved my life. It still hurt like hell.

"You okay, old man?" Yuri sounded concerned.

"It's only a flesh wound," I said in a John Cleese voice.

Yuri cut the tape, freeing me. I got up and he taped Tracy into the chair. He taped Bruno, still unconscious, into his. I picked up the gun. I needed to free Gina.

In the hallway, two goons were lying face down

bound and gagged. They weren't moving.

"How did you do it?"

Yuri answered, "As you suggested, I put chloral hydrate in everything to drink. Juice in the fridge, coffee maker, water jug, even vodka. I have blade in my shoe for cut ties. Viktor broke his bindings. I heard one guard fall, then the other tried to help him. Both out."

Tracy yelled, "You didn't tell me about that, you bastard."

"It must have slipped my mind."

I stepped into the concrete room. Gina was moving slightly. I took the black bag off her head. She looked at me without recognition.

"Help me with her." I nodded to Viktor. He cut the ties and picked her up in his arms as though she weighed nothing.

"Put her on the bed in the other room."

He carried her into the master bedroom and lay her gently on the bed. I went to the bathroom and got a damp towel. I wiped her face and hands.

"Gina, it's Chan. Can you talk?"

She turned her head slowly and looked at me. "Chan…what are you doing here."

"I came to rescue you."

Gina's eyes didn't focus right. She looked unhurt but confused. She was pale and seemed to have lost some weight. "They made me take…pills. Did you catch Bruno?"

"Yes, he's tied to a chair over there. He's unconscious."

I took Tracy's cell phone off her belt and redialed the last number. A phone rang in Bruno's pants. I hung up. The attack in Bamfield must have been her way of convincing me we were a team. That and the sex...

I felt like the fool I was. I should have felt triumphant but the damage to my ego was extreme.

I used Tracy's phone to call Andy and let him know we were alright. I went to the kitchen and got Gina a bottle of water, sealed. She was beginning to look a bit better. I keyed in a secret URL to the browser and downloaded the Saga app into Tracy's phone.

"What happened?" Saga said when I started the app.

"You were shot. At least the phone was. It was destroyed. You saved my life."

While I tended to Gina, I thought about what to do with the four criminals. I decided that we would just leave them there, then call the police. I'd tell the truth about the rescue, more or less. I expected the police would be angry with us for taking vigilante action, but I doubted if we'd be prosecuted.

Tracy was sobbing softly to herself. I felt sorry for her, then I looked at Gina and all sympathy for Tracy vanished. Bruno was moving his head and mumbling. The drug was wearing off.

Gina sat up. She looked around and saw Bruno. She suddenly leaped up and pushed me aside, grabbing the pistol off the bed where I had put it down. In one smooth motion, she stepped over to Bruno, raised the pistol, and shot him in the forehead. Blood spattered the wall and the chair fell backward. She was turning to shoot Tracy when Viktor grabbed her arm and aimed it for the ceiling. The second shot went wild.

*Memo to self: Do. Not. Cross. Gina. Ever.*

Viktor gently took the pistol away and sat her on the bed. She put her hands to her face and cried. "He raped me. Bully raped me. Every day."

I took Gina in my arms and she sobbed into my shoulder for a very long time. After a while, a nagging memory came to the front of my mind.

"Tiggy?"

She nodded.

# 28 THE RESTAURANT AT THE END OF THE UNIVERSE

The Laughing Oyster was the best restaurant on Malaspina Inlet. It was also the only restaurant on Malaspina inlet. It was a month after the rescue. Saga made the reservations and organized a dinner so Gina could express her gratitude.

Ollie and Kimi arrived in the red Alfa Romeo. Charlie and Desdemona were just behind in the old Rolls-Royce. Blue Rose was tied up at the dock. Aphrodite was anchored nearby, as was Adonis. Levi, Yuri, and Viktor sent their regrets. Feinman was planning to come but hadn't arrived yet.

Gina and I had sailed Blue Rose up from Vancouver. On the way, I got to know her properly. The night at the Empress was a show she put on to reward me for saving her life all those years before. The real Gina was down to earth and lots of fun, with a wicked sense of humor. And she could really sail Blue Rose.

The crews of Aphrodite and Adonis sailed there too, leaving a day later than us and arriving ahead. It turned out Peter Tombolo was an innocent dupe. He didn't even know Bruno, Tracy faked the call.

He and Gina were still friends.

I introduced Gina to my gang and she introduced them to her crew. Billy took me aside and apologized for firing me. It seems Tracy had emailed him some made-up story that I was just in it for the money.

We took over the whole restaurant. The chef

created a special menu with many types of oysters, prawns, and scallops. Rack of lamb, Alaska black cod, wild salmon, and even steak—all were available. Gina had Veuve Clicquot 2004, Chateau Lafite-Rothschild, Domaine Coche-Dury and other fine wines brought up from her yacht.

When everyone had full glasses, Gina stood up. She looked amazing in a simple emerald green dress. Her hair hung straight to just below her shoulders. She wore pearl in each ear and a single strand around her neck.

"I want to propose a toast to all of you who contributed to my rescue. I particularly want to thank Chan, who despite his many flaws—I'm preparing a list—never gave up on finding me. He saved my life for the second time. And just as important, his assistant Saga, without whose ideas and actions Chan and I might not be alive. I still have some legal issues to sort out, but my lawyer assures me it will be alright."

She raised her glass, followed by much clinking and laughter.

"Now I want Saga to make a speech. She knows the full story better than I do."

Gina sat down. I was on her right. On her left were an LCD monitor and two speakers. The screen lit up and a face appeared. It was a face that looked like it could be Gina's sister, except for bright blue eyes which seemed to glow from within. The lips were dark red and moved in perfect sync with Saga's British voice.

"It started with a dream..."

GRAHAME SHANNON

## THE END

# EPILOGUE

Gina Lee was charged with manslaughter. After hearing her story and witness statements, the provincial attorney decided not to prosecute. No jury would have convicted her.

Tracy Wagner pleaded guilty to kidnapping, as did her two henchmen. She was sentenced to two years in jail. Tracy claimed Bruno Beckson was the mastermind, and the motive was stock manipulation. He wasn't around to contradict her. Personally, I think it was all about revenge on Gina.

The Aphrodite crew and I shared the salvage money we got from the Adonis. Gina decided to sell her yacht and keep a lower profile in future. She said she preferred sailing with me on Blue Rose. We made plans to spend a few weeks together each year.

Gina found out she was Tombolo's older half-sister. Their mother, by then deceased, was Japanese from Isahiya. His father was an American soldier. She concluded her mother must have somehow got her into the Omura refugee camp for Vietnamese orphans. Apart from that, the Japanese connections were coincidental.

I found another two hundred thousand or so in my brokerage account. Apparently, Saga went long on Gina's stock before news of her release hit the media. Plans have been made to restore the Mustang and Blue Rose.

# NOTE

This is a work of fiction. Most of the locations are real, but the story and principal characters are fictional.

British Columbia and Alaska are filled with little-known but spectacular coastal landscapes. The sea in between is the mariner's highway.

I have taken some liberties with the geography of Lancelot Inlet and Barkley Sound. The maps are not to be used for navigation.

# ABOUT THE AUTHOR

Grahame Shannon was born in Grenada, some time ago. His many careers have had widely varying degrees of success. He has been a boat builder, a naval architect, and a software developer. In the 1980s he developed Autoship, one of the first 3D CAD systems for yacht and ship design. Most recently he has devoted himself to sailing the BC coast and writing short stories and novels.

Made in the USA
Charleston, SC
16 February 2017